JENNIFER S. ALDERSON

Death by Baguette

A Valentine's Day Murder in Paris

For Philip, my forever valentine.

Contents

1	The Big One	1
2	Hot Yoga	6
3	Heavenly Strawberries	11
4	Circling the City of Love	15
5	Paris Syndrome	19
6	What Was I To You?	25
7	Cruising the River Seine	28
8	Love Stones	35
9	Bad Vibes	40
10	Jardin des Tuileries	44
11	So Much for Seeing the Louvre	51
12	Rabies Shots and Art History	53
13	Fountains and Food Markets	56
14	Last-Minute Changes	66
15	Travel Time	69
16	Lana Gets Curious	74
17	Jardin des Plantes	78
18	Kicked Out of the Moulin Rouge	88
19	Baking a Baguette	94
20	Picnicking under the Eiffel Tower	97
21	The Baker Killed My Husband!	106
22	Death by Baguette?	109
23	Chartres Cathedral	117
24	A Liar and a Cheat	123
25	Persons of Interest	126
26	Museum Rodin	131

27 A Shark in Loose-Fitting Clothes   136
28 Enlisting Help from an Old Friend   142
29 The Inspector Returns   147
30 Afternoon Tea at Versailles   151
31 Do Fish Sunbathe?   164
32 Perfect Day for a Picnic   173
Acknowledgments   179
About the Author   180
Death by Windmill: A Mother's Day Murder in Amsterdam   182

1

The Big One

February 1—Seattle, Washington

Lana Hansen awoke in a panic, certain Seattle's long-anticipated, catastrophic earthquake was finally happening. Seymour jumped up on her chest, meowing in fright, as the sharp, tearing sound rippling through her ceiling increased in intensity.

Lana grabbed ahold of her cat and raced outside, scared for her upstairs neighbor's safety, as well as their own. Their two-story farmhouse was one of the oldest wooden homes left in this neighborhood, and Lana was certain it would not survive the "Big One" seismologists had been warning locals about for decades.

Once outside, she surveyed her rented home, surprised to see that the siding was intact. In fact, nothing seemed to be shaking or moving, not even the weeping willow in their front yard. And the piercing noise was gone, too.

Filled with adrenaline and uncertainty, Lana rang Dotty Thompson's doorbell, wanting to make sure her upstairs neighbor had survived the initial shock.

Moments later, Dotty opened the door, her face covered in a thick sheen of sweat. "Lana, why are you in your pajamas? Where are your shoes? You better get in here before you catch a cold," she huffed, clearly out of breath.

She was dressed in a leopard-skin spandex top and bright pink tights. A pink headband and leopard-skin legwarmers completed the ensemble.

Around Dotty's legs danced her dogs, Chipper and Rodney—or her "boys" as she preferred to call them. They were dressed in matching pink headbands with tiny leopard-print armbands around their front paws.

"I think we just had an earthquake!" Lana said, frozen in place. "You'd better come outside, in case there are aftershocks."

"An earthquake? Are you sure? I didn't feel anything moving, but then I was doing jumping jacks just now," Dotty said as she began springing up and down, the old wooden floorboards groaning and creaking under her weight.

Lana leaned against the doorway. "Were you doing them in your living room?"

"Yes, why?"

Dotty's living room was directly above Lana's bedroom. *So that was the thundering noise*, she realized. Her rush of adrenaline subsided as quickly as it arrived. Lana shivered a little and stepped inside Dotty's hallway. "Never mind about the earthquake. It must have been a crazy dream."

When she followed Dotty into her living room, Lana could immediately feel sweat forming on her brow. "Why is it so hot in here?"

"I turned the heater way up. The warmth is supposed to help burn more calories while doing yoga."

"Why are you exercising so early, anyway? It's not even six," Lana asked as she dropped onto Dotty's couch, Seymour still in her arms. At least, until Rodney and Chipper bolted onto the couch, scaring her cat off.

"Chipper! Rodney! Where are your manners?" Dotty admonished her pets, then waddled off to find Seymour.

The pug and Jack Russell terrier growled at each other as they both tried to climb onto Lana's legs. "Okay, boys, I have enough hands and lap for both of you." Lana petted their backs until they settled into a truce with both of their heads on her lap and a body on each side of her legs.

Dotty soon returned with Lana's cat in her arms and sat down next to her. Seymour flicked his tail against Lana's arm but remained in Dotty's lap.

"I must have overdone it salsa dancing last night because my back sure is complaining. Willow's coming over for an emergency yoga session to help me work out the kinks."

"That's nice of her. So did Willow tell Jane yet, or is she still planning on surprising her?" Lana asked, hoping it was the former rather than the latter.

Dotty had arranged for them to join Lana's next tour—a lovers-only trip to Paris in mid-February. As sweet as it was that Willow wanted to surprise Jane with a week-long vacation to one of the most romantic cities in the world, Lana knew Jane would not appreciate the surprise element. In fact, she suspected that a surprise trip would push Jane over the edge, rather than rekindling their romance.

Jane was a wonderful doctor who had just opened up her own practice and regarded her patients as family, staying on call at all hours for them. Yet she was so dedicated to them, Lana wondered whether Jane would ever make time to start her own, despite saying she wanted to do so.

Willow, on the other hand, had made it clear after her thirty-fifth birthday party last month that she was ready to start in-vitro fertilization this year— but only if Jane agreed to work less. The ultimatum made Jane feel as if she had to choose between her career and children. Both women were stubborn and had dug in their heels, and Lana feared that no resolution was in sight.

Dotty sighed and shook her head. "Willow seems convinced that this trip would be best as a surprise. She thinks Jane wouldn't agree to go, otherwise. She's trying to get one of her doctor friends to cover for her, so Jane won't be able to say no."

"Oh yes she will. Jane may be small and quiet, but she is no pushover. You sure don't want to get on her bad side," Lana said.

"I agree with you there. Last week, I saw her chew out a parking valet for slamming her door too hard. I mean, the windows did shake a bit, but nothing broke or cracked. I swear, he was twice her size but was on the verge of tears by the time she got done with him," Dotty said. "I know you aren't convinced, Lana, but I do think this trip will help their relationship. If they are serious about having a child together, they need to make time to talk things out. A week in Paris might just do the trick. Heck, a week in Timbuktu would probably work, too, as long as they really listen to each other."

Lana started to respond when the doorbell rang.

Dotty set Seymour on the couch next to her and rose. "Speak of the devil. Since you're here, why don't you stay and join in?"

"Sure, why not?" Lana stretched her arms out over her lap, jostling the dogs. They grumbled in irritation, but both stayed put. With her hectic tour schedule, she hadn't done yoga or any other regular exercise for months. The walking tours kept her fit, as did running around helping her guests, but she missed the feeling of burning muscles and sweat on her forehead.

Lana gave Rodney and Chipper a hard scratch on the back then slowly rose. Both the pug and Jack Russell terrier rolled off her lap and curled into balls next to Seymour.

When Dotty led Willow back into the room, Lana stood still, unsure as how to greet her friend.

Willow set her rolled-up yoga mat down and put her hands on her hips. "Howdy, stranger! It's good to see you." She stood on her toes to wrap her arms around Lana's neck.

Lana hugged her back, careful not to pull on Willow's long braids. A wave of shame rolled over her. It wasn't that she had been consciously avoiding Willow since returning from Berlin three weeks earlier, but it was a fact that she had not dropped by her friend's apartment or work as often as she usually did. Willow and Jane were fighting more frequently it was hard for Lana to be around them without taking sides. And the last thing she wanted to do was get involved in their baby discussion.

Truth be told, it wasn't just their squabbling that kept her away. She had recently re-entered the dating scene and met a man with potential, which made her even more sensitive to Willow and Jane's troubles. It was hard to be around a couple fighting when she was in the euphoric phase of a new relationship.

"Willow, it's great to see you, too. I'm so sorry I didn't stay until the end of Jane's birthday party. Were you at the restaurant much longer?" Lana had immediately said yes when Chad, her new beau, asked her out to dinner, only to later realize that Jane's birthday was the same night. In an attempt to combine both, Lana had asked Chad if he would instead meet her at a nearby bar for a nightcap afterwards. However, Lana had forgotten how large Jane's family was; dinners with them took significantly longer than normal, and so she'd had to cut out of Jane's party before the other guests were finished.

Willow pursed her lips and looked away. "No. Her mother started in about kids and how we should hurry up and adopt. Apparently Jane hadn't told her we were going to try IVF first."

Ouch, Lana thought. Jane told her mother everything; excluding this big news was not a good sign. "Well, I'm sure she had a reason for waiting to tell…"

"Okay, girls, enough chitchat." Dotty clapped her hands together as she started to jog in place. "I'm all warmed up, and my back is killing me. What do we do first, Willow?"

Willow unfurled her mat across from Dotty. "We salute the sun."

"Oh, I know this one," Dotty exclaimed, standing in the starting position with her feet together and her palms touching in front of her chest.

Lana stood between her friends and copied their stance.

"Now, ladies, let's do this!"

2

Hot Yoga

Thirty sweaty minutes later, Dotty threw herself onto the couch and dabbed her forehead dry. "That was quite the workout! Thanks, Willow, my back feels as good as new."

"That's great, Dotty. But maybe you should take it easy next time you go dancing and let your muscles get used to moving again," Willow said, as she rolled up her mat.

"I think you're right about that. I'll have to work my way up to a full night of dancing." Dotty kept wiping at the sweat streaming down her cheeks. Lana wasn't surprised; the apartment felt like a sauna. "Say, Lana, there's lemon water in the fridge. Would you mind pouring us all a glass?"

"No problem." After Lana returned with glasses and a pitcher, Dotty polished off two cups in quick succession and let out a tiny burp. "Phew, that's better."

"Since I'm here, why don't I take the boys out for their walk?" Lana asked. "After I pull on some warmer clothes and shoes," she added. Fremont was quite an alternative neighborhood, meaning no one would give her a second glance, but there was still a frosty chill in the morning air.

"Sounds good to me. Let me get their sweaters on them. It's still too cold outside to go without them."

Lana chuckled. Dotty seemed to forget that normal house pets didn't have a closet full of clothes. Lana often wondered what her landlord would think of all the naked animals she passed on her daily walks. If Dotty had her way, all animals would be clothed.

Dotty pushed herself up, then searched around in her sewing bag, stuffed in the corner of her couch. "Here they are. I just love Sally's designs. She is so darn creative; I don't know what I would do without her." She held up a dog sweater for Lana and Willow to see. It was a pattern of terriers and hearts circling the animal's torso.

"It's adorable," both gushed with sincerity.

Last year, Dotty and her friend Sally had begun knitting doggy sweaters for Doggone Gorgeous—their line of canine clothing. They'd sold so well that the ladies already had a long waiting list and were roping any and all knitting friends into the business.

Their creations for Purrfect Fit, a clothing line for cats, were equally adorable, though sadly less popular. Apparently Dotty was one of the few who could get felines into clothes.

Willow rose from the comfortable couch and grabbed her mat. "I better head over to my studio. I have a class starting in twenty minutes." Luckily Willows Bend, her yoga studio, was only a few streets away, in the heart of Fremont.

As Dotty pulled the sweaters onto her patient dogs, she said, "Before you go, we should talk about Paris. What did Jane say? Or have you not told her yet?"

"The doctor I asked to cover for Jane wanted to talk with her about her patients first, so I had to tell her."

"How did she react?" Lana cringed in anticipation.

Willow looked away. "Honestly, not as badly as I had expected."

"Is she willing to join you, or…" Dotty didn't dare finish her question.

"Yes, because 'I put her on the spot and she doesn't want to lose face by saying no,'" Willow cited, her face a mask of neutrality.

Lana could imagine that it was a far more spirited conversation than her friend's demeanor indicated.

"I don't know why she's embarrassed that I asked that doctor friend. Last summer, she covered for him for two weeks while he was on vacation. I don't understand what the big deal is."

Your partner is a control freak, Lana wanted to say, but didn't dare. When they were not fighting, they were the most normal couple she knew and the easiest to be around. Lana knew they loved each other deeply and could get through this current crisis, but it still hurt her to see her friends suffering so.

"You two really need this time to reconnect, that's all," Dotty reassured Willow.

Lana grabbed her friend's shoulders. "We're going to Paris together next week!"

"Paris!" Willow squealed. Lana knew her friends had been to Japan several times to visit with Jane's maternal grandparents, but they had never been to Europe. "I can't wait! It looks so beautiful and romantic in all those films. The River Seine, the Eiffel Tower and Louvre, baguettes with brie, and chocolatey crêpes... I can hardly wait." Willow sighed dreamily.

"It's going to be great," Lana agreed. Paris did seem so romantic in films. *If only Chad was free to join me,* she thought, then quickly scolded herself. They had only been on three dates. Accompanying her to Paris while she was working was probably not the smartest move right now. If anything, the weeks apart would enable her to separate her excitement at being in a new relationship from her true feelings for him. Though right now, the idea of dating Chad for the long term seemed pretty wonderful.

Dotty patted Willow's shoulder. "I'm so glad you'll be able to join the tour. And it might be good to have two friends around, in case Randy needs some extra help or attention."

Lana nodded in agreement. She was a little miffed that Dotty had asked her to train a new tour guide so soon. This would only be her fourth tour as a Wanderlust guide, and she barely felt qualified as the assistant. Now she was going to be the lead guide and trainer. She only hoped Randy was easygoing and quick to learn.

Lana knew Dotty wouldn't have asked her to do this if she'd had any other choice. A string of great reviews about her specialty tours garnered Wanderlust Tours extra attention online, which resulted in a regional travel magazine featuring the company prominently in an article. Lana wasn't surprised. For those who could afford it, it was the ultimate tour. Wanderlust Tours specialized in creating dream vacations for rich Seattleites long on cash but short on time. Dotty even allowed guests to request that day trips or special tours be added to the itinerary, making each trip unique.

Within a week of the article's publication, almost all of the tours for the coming year were booked out. The lovers-only tour to Paris was one exception, which Lana suspected had to do with Dotty's decision to also give it a gourmet theme this year. When three couples signed up immediately, Dotty had been certain her new idea was a success. But six months later, only one more couple had shown interest, leaving two empty reservations, which were now being filled by Jane and Willow. Dotty preferred to keep her tours full, if only to appease the hotel and restaurant owners she used.

"Having you two there will help balance out the group, as well. Otherwise the last couple that signed up may have felt left out. From what I understand, the three that booked straightaway are all friends. They sure are particular, too; they keep requesting changes to the itinerary."

"Really, this late? We are meeting up in Paris next week."

"I know, but you know my policy is to do all I can to make my guests' wishes come true. They do pay a pretty penny for our trips, and I want them to be satisfied."

"What did they ask for?"

"The first addition is a tour of the botanical gardens. Apparently the three women all volunteer at a horticulture club in Volunteer Park."

"I didn't know they had botanical gardens in Paris."

"Truth be told, I didn't either. But it's supposed to be quite large and old. It should be interesting. If all of your guests enjoy it, we can add it to our list of optional extras for our Paris trips."

"Sounds good. What else do they want to do?"

"Yesterday they asked that we add a baking workshop."

"As in desserts?" Lana's mouth began to water just thinking about all those delicious pastries and cakes the French were known for.

"No, bread. They want to learn how to make real French bread, you know, those baguettes."

"Oh, that sounds wonderful, too! I hope it wasn't too much trouble for you."

"Yes, well, I was lucky the baker she requested was willing to create a special workshop for our guests. His normal classes were fully booked."

"It sounds like we are going to have a busy tour!"

"It is a bit fuller than I had originally planned, but there is still more free time built into this tour than the normal ones. After all, it is a Valentine-themed tour," Dotty cackled. "Even with the additional extras, our guests should have plenty of time to sneak off on their own."

Lana blushed but tittered along. A few months ago, she would have felt too rejected to laugh. But now that she'd started dating again, she could appreciate the need for romance.

"Just to be clear, nobody is required to do anything. I would rather reserve too many seats than disappoint our guests."

"That's awfully generous of you, Dotty."

"Yeah, well, I guess I'm a generous kind of person. Why don't you get some warmer clothes on while I get my boys dressed." Dotty stretched her arms over her head and yawned. "Now that my back isn't complaining, I feel a nap coming on."

3

Heavenly Strawberries

February 8—Seattle, Washington

"These are heavenly," Lana gushed, while savoring the most delicious chocolate-covered strawberry she had ever eaten. The fruit was dipped in dark chocolate and rolled in crushed cashews. She took another bite of the exquisite dessert in her hand, letting the sweetness roll over her tongue. It was the perfect end to a perfect Valentine's picnic with her new boyfriend, Chad.

She picked up a cluster of chocolatey blueberries and marveled at their decorations. "I'd heard of chocolate-covered strawberries, but I didn't know you could dip blueberries, raspberries, or orange slices in chocolate. I figured they would dissolve."

"Not if the sauce is at the right temperature. I do love how the tartness of the blueberries brings out the sweetness of the chocolate," Chad said, popping one strewn with vanilla chips into his mouth.

They were sitting on a blanket in her living room, watching the rain cascade down as they finished their lunch. Because of a sudden downpour, they'd had to cut their romantic picnic at Gas Works Park short. Luckily the rain started after they had finished their scrumptious appetizers and main course. Chad had picked up the food on his way over; he knew all of the best restaurants in town. They say the way to a man's heart is through his stomach, but Lana knew it applied to women, as well.

"It's too bad we won't be able to spend Valentine's Day together," he said, feeding her the last raspberry.

"Next year we'll have to go away together, just the two of us," Lana responded, then reddened when she realized she had spoken the words aloud. They'd only been together three weeks, nine hours, and forty-seven minutes. Maybe making plans for next year's Valentine's Day was a bit premature.

"Sounds good to me," Chad murmured, to her great relief.

Lana was slightly disappointed she had to work on the most romantic day of the year, instead of spending it with her new friend. Unfortunately, with Wanderlust being so busy, Lana knew none of the other guides were free to take her place. And if she asked for a week off, Dotty would want to know why.

It was also so early in their relationship that Lana hadn't mentioned Chad to any of her friends, figuring she would tell them about him once she was certain they were going to be a couple. She still had trouble calling Chad her boyfriend, even in her own mind. Her ex-husband's betrayal after nine years of marriage had been so unexpected, she wanted to take it real slow until she could get used to trusting a man again.

It was only after her first tour in Budapest that Lana had mustered the courage to start dating again. Back then, she'd thought her erratic schedule would make dating difficult, until Willow showed her a new website called Seattle Singles. Thanks to its app, she could check the website from anywhere in the world and make contact with potential suitors through a secure mailbox. Her first attempt at creating an online profile was shot down by Dotty and Willow as being too boring. They helped her spice up her personal information, even suggesting she fib a bit and say she worked at a travel agency, but not as a guide. As much as she hated lying, even Lana realized that a job that took her out of town so often might scare away some potential dates.

Chad had been one of the first to respond with a flirty message, and he remained one of the most intriguing suitors so far. According to his profile, he was a website developer who often traveled around the country giving training sessions. Smart and well-traveled sounded perfect to Lana, especially once she took a look at his photos. He was fifty-nine, thus a bit older than she had expected to date, but quite good-looking in a distinguished way. She elected not to get hung up on the age difference but instead to simply enjoy flirting again. Right now, finding someone who was kind and whom she could connect with was more important than meeting someone of any particular age.

She and Chad started out by chatting about travel, yet his daily messages quickly become more flirtatious. Yet after weeks of online chatting, he still hadn't asked her out. The day before Lana was to fly home from Berlin, she suggested they meet up.

Her heart had skipped a beat when he immediately responded with "What time should I come over to your place?"

Since her return three weeks ago, they had spoken daily and seen each other three times. There was something so charismatic and warm about Chad, she could feel herself falling for him, despite the fact that they had just met.

Today's picnic was only reinforcing those feelings. Chad was leaning in to kiss her, his mouth almost to hers, when a loud beeping noise disrupted them.

"Is that your neighbor's fire alarm?" he asked, looking up towards Lana's ceiling.

She sniffed the air for smoke. "I don't smell anything. Dotty must be cooking one of her pot roasts again. She's a wonderful person, but a horrible cook."

Before either could rise to see what was making the noise, the beeping stopped.

"Sorry, where were we?" Chad smiled at her as he leaned forward. Lana closed her eyes in anticipation, when the rattle of chains followed by the sound of something heavy being lifted made Chad pull back again.

"It sounds like it's coming from outside." He rose to look out the only window with a view of the narrow street running along her house. She joined him at the window as his BMW rode past, on the back of a tow truck.

"My car! It's being towed!" Chad raced out of Lana's apartment and chased after his Beemer.

Moments later he slunk back inside. "I can't believe it. I didn't see any 'No Parking' signs."

Lana sighed. "Did you park on the left-hand side of the street, next to that gigantic fir tree? There's a fire hydrant there, but it's partially hidden by the tree's trunk. I bet you didn't see it." Lana felt like a fool. She hadn't thought to mention the fire hydrant when Chad arrived this morning. And they'd turned to the right when they left her house to go picnicking, not left. Otherwise, she could have warned him.

"I'm going to have to leave, Lana. I need to get my car back before I go to that conference in Pittsburgh tomorrow." Chad pulled her close and kissed her. "This is not how I hoped to spend our last night together."

"That's right. You're leaving tomorrow, aren't you?" Lana said with a tinge of regret. "We won't see each other for two weeks. I'm flying to Tokyo before you return," she lied. To explain her absence without admitting her real job, she had told him that she was being sent to Japan to scope out potential new destinations. She hated lying to Chad and knew that she would have to tell him the truth one day, if their relationship became serious. But considering this was only their third date, she figured she had time to think up a plausible reason for misleading him.

Chad brushed his lips against hers. His touch sent tingles of joy through her body. "In two weeks, we'll have another picnic. This time with a better ending, I hope."

When Chad's cab arrived minutes later, he pulled on his coat and kissed her cheek. Lana's heart fluttered in longing. After months of being single, it was really nice to be dating again. *It is only two weeks*, she reminded herself, as he walked to the waiting cab. Lana had been single for months. She could definitely survive on her own for fourteen days.

4

Circling the City of Love

February 12—Day One of the Wanderlust Tour in Paris, France

Their plane flew over the outskirts of Paris as they circled to their runway at Charles de Gaulle Airport. Lana gazed out the window, excited to visit the city of lights and love. It was early morning, so Lana knew the iconic Eiffel Tower wouldn't be lit up, but she swore she spotted the slender monument far in the distance.

A tap on the shoulder interrupted her sightseeing. She pulled out her earbuds and smiled at the grumpy stewardess standing in the aisle holding a trash bag.

"Are you finished?" she asked, nodding towards the half-eaten breakfast sandwich on Lana's foldout tray.

"Yeah, thanks." Lana leaned over Randy Wright, her seatmate and fellow Wanderlust Tours guide, and threw the remaining food into the bag. She couldn't bring herself to eat the rest of that spongy sandwich, not when she was a mere hour away from having access to real French crêpes, baguettes, and chocolate croissants. Simply thinking of those gooey warm pastries made her mouth water.

"The Musée d'Orsay doesn't interest me at all. The Louvre's worth a visit, but I don't want to spend all my free time in art museums," Jane declared resolutely. She and Willow were sitting in the row behind her and Randy.

Lana knew that Jane suffered terribly from motion sickness and was taking all sorts of herbal remedies to try to lessen it—with mixed success. Still, their constant bickering was the reason she had put the earbuds in. Well, at least one of them.

Randy was smiling at her while trying to make eye contact. Lana groaned internally. As much as she appreciated Randy's enthusiasm for his new job, his endless stream of questions had grown quite trying five hours into the flight. Nobody had been there to hold her hand during her first tour to Budapest, and it had worked out. *Well, except for the two deaths*, Lana thought, but that hadn't been her fault.

Since then, she had spent two wonderful weeks in Costa Rica and another two in Berlin leading groups around, and the worst thing to happen on those trips was an infected splinter. Even though this was only her fourth trip, Lana was beginning to feel as if leading tours was what she was meant to do. The guests could sometimes be trying, but most were wonderful people truly interested in learning more about the countries they were visiting. Her main responsibility was to tag along on their day trips, meaning she was experiencing the same sights and sounds as they were. Yet instead of shelling out thousands of dollars for the privilege, she was paid to be there. What could be better than that?

Those first few hours of their eleven-hour flight, Lana had happily answered Randy's inquiries about his responsibilities during the tour. Any lulls in their conversation were filled in with snippets of Willow and Jane's bickering. Despite Willow's assurances that everything would be fine, Jane was not pleased with a surprise trip to Paris. In fact, she was downright livid. The only reason she was on the plane was to save face with the doctor whom Willow had asked to cover Jane's practice.

So far, all of Willow's suggestions as to how they could fill their pockets of free time were met with disdain and negativity from Jane. What was happening to her friends? Up until a month ago, they were the most stable and loving couple she knew. She hoped their baby wishes would not destroy their marriage.

Part of Lana was dying to step in and attempt to defuse the situation. But she didn't dare do so. These were two good friends, not clients. During their tour, she would have no choice but to say something if their squabbling affected the others. Keeping the group spirit positive was an important part of her job.

But for now, she chose to ignore her friends. Earlier in the flight, when Randy's questions seemed to be winding down, she had feigned tiredness and pulled out her headphones.

She began popping her headphones back in when Randy cleared his throat loudly. His eyes sparkled in anticipation. The man was eager, too much so. Especially considering he had not slept, instead spending his quiet time pouring over all of the travel guides Dotty had given him.

"Did you sleep well?" Randy asked.

"It was good to doze off a little," Lana acknowledged while sitting up properly in her chair. She stretched out her back, careful not to hit her knuckles on the overhead bins.

Lana nodded to the books stacked up on his foldout tray. "Which one would you recommend I read first?" she asked.

Randy went white as a sheet. "You mean you haven't read these yet? I thought this was your first time in Paris, too."

"I'm teasing you, Randy," she said with a laugh, hoping he would lighten up a little. High-strung was not a good quality for a tour guide.

He looked confused, then broke into a grin. "Sure, right. You'll have to forgive me. I am pretty nervous about this gig. It's been months since I've led any group, and never older clients through a city before." Randy had ruddy cheeks from being outside so much of his life, a trim figure, long wavy red hair, and strong biceps. If she had been single, she might even think he was cute, in a goofy sort of way.

He was one of three new hires this month and was the first to respond to Dotty's advertisement for seasonal guides. He had led groups of mountaineers up Mount Rainier until an accident shattered his right leg and confidence. After several surgeries and extensive physical therapy, he was able to walk properly, though with a slight limp. However, guiding groups up the mountain was out of the question.

Dotty said Randy was quite experienced but would need a lot of encouragement, which was why she'd placed him with Lana. Lana could empathize with his uncertainty. After being wrongfully fired from her job at the *Seattle Chronicle*, it had taken her years to find her way again.

"Ladies and gentlemen, we are beginning our approach to Paris. Please return to your seats and fasten your seatbelts. It is sunny and sixty-five degrees Fahrenheit, which is unusually warm for this time of year. Local time is 9:14 a.m. We hope you enjoy your stay in the City of Love."

Lana was thrilled to hear the weather was better than in Seattle and no rain was expected.

Randy was struggling to get his books back into his day pack. The zipper appeared to be stuck on a bit of fabric and wouldn't budge. As he wrestled with his luggage, their section's stewardess approached. Unfortunately, she seemed to be having a bad day and was not in the mood for his delay.

"Your bag needs to go in the overhead bin now," she said, her tone stern.

"Gosh, I'm a little slow today, aren't I?" Randy chuckled in a self-deprecating way as he patiently worked the zipper loose. "I sure do apologize for holding you up." What could have been delivered sarcastically was said with such sincerity that the stewardess's eyes widened in shock. After a moment's hesitation, she even cracked a smile.

Randy finally freed the zipper, closing his day pack with a flourish. "Now, let's get this naughty bag back to where it belongs so you can do your work," he said.

The stewardess helped him close the overhead bin, blushing as their hands touched. "Enjoy your stay in Paris, sir," she said sincerely, before taking her seat.

Randy hummed as he sat down and buckled up.

Lana looked at him with new eyes. "How did you do that?" she whispered, afraid the stewardess might hear her. "She's been horrible this entire flight."

Randy shrugged. "I don't know. Just by being polite, I guess."

If Randy could put that sour stewardess at ease, this week won't be as challenging as I anticipated, Lana thought.

5

Paris Syndrome

The Charles de Gaulle Airport was a hive of activity. Lana, Randy, Willow, and Jane followed the signs to baggage claim, allowing themselves to be pushed along with the crowd. After recovering their luggage, it took them longer than expected to find the exit and the hotel's shuttle bus stop.

The hotel they were staying at was apparently quite large because almost thirty passengers stood waiting for the free shuttle bus. Lana knew her clients were here somewhere, but she only had names and passport numbers, no photos. Technically, the tour didn't start until their welcome dinner, this time on a boat touring the River Seine. Lana couldn't wait.

A string of minivans soon arrived and whisked them away from the airport and towards the center of Paris. Lana's vintage suitcase was one of the largest, she noticed, as the driver struggled to get it into the van. As much as she loved the old leather case, it was bulky and heavy. *A smaller suitcase might be in order*, she thought, *preferably one with wheels*.

While their minivan driver beeped and swore at the traffic, Lana gazed out the window, shocked to see beggars and stray animals amongst the well-dressed Parisians crowding the city's sidewalks. The architecture was grand and imposing, but there were heaps of garbage piled on many street corners.

On the plane ride over, Lana had read an article in the in-flight magazine about "Paris syndrome," a psychological disorder that primarily affected Japanese tourists. Because an idealized version of all things French was so popular in Japan, some tourists' experiences of the real Paris differed so greatly from their romanticized notions that they had mini-mental breakdowns resulting in hallucinations and delusions. Approximately twenty Japanese tourists a year had to be evacuated by their embassy. Though she had laughed a little on the plane, she could understand it now. She was going to need time to comprehend that the Paris she was now driving through was also the birthplace of so much world-class art and culture.

When their van turned onto the Place de la Concorde, Lana gazed up in wonder at the Egyptian obelisk standing on an island in the middle of the heavy, chaotic traffic. Across a swath of green, Lana could see the morning sun reflecting off the top of a glass pyramid—the entrance to the massive Louvre Museum. When they crossed the River Seine via the Pont de la Concorde to a street named Quai d'Orsay, Lana swore she could see Notre Dame. Lana had to pinch herself to keep from squealing. They were really in Paris!

"This place is incredible," she murmured to Randy, getting a nod in response. He also seemed to be captivated by the world-famous monuments they were driving by. Slowly they wound their way through several side streets to Hotel Seine. It was on the corner of a busy street a few blocks from the river it was named for. It was stately and regal, with scrollwork covering the old stone façade. Their rooms were not large but were beautifully decorated, and the fantastic views alone were worth the stay. Lana opened up her window and stared out at the iconic Eiffel Tower in the distance, sighing in delight.

"*Très magnifique*," Lana mumbled, one of the few phrases she could still recall from her high school French lessons.

She tipped the bellboy generously, not concerned about getting a receipt. Incidental expenses were part of the job and the reason why Dotty had given her a supply of euros before leaving Seattle. As the bellboy bowed his way out the door in gratitude, Randy walked around him and entered without asking.

"This hotel is incredible," he gushed. "Your room looks just like mine." He walked around, taking in the chandelier, antique furnishings, four-post bed, and sumptuous draperies, before stopping at her balcony's doors. "You do have a better view, though. My room looks out over the river and Louvre."

Lana pushed her irritation at his intrusion aside and joined him at the window. "That sounds pretty amazing, too."

"It's not bad. Say, what are you going to do before showtime?" Randy asked.

"The group doesn't meet up until 5 p.m., so we have plenty of time to explore Paris on our own," she said, emphasizing the last phrase.

"Friends told me about a rock wall I have to climb. Would you like to go bouldering with me?" Randy asked, his tone pleading.

"Oh gosh, thanks for the offer, but I'm not much of a climber. I would rather take some time for myself before we meet up with our group. Once the tour starts, the guests are going to keep us quite busy."

Randy looked like a puppy dog who'd just been scolded. "Sure, no problem. Enjoy your free time. Could we walk down to the lobby together tonight, when it's time to meet the guests?"

"That sounds great. Why don't you knock at a quarter to five?"

"Perfect." Randy's face lit up. Lana was glad he was easy to please, at least.

He turned and walked back to his room. Before Lana could close her door, Willow appeared. She pulled her friend into a big hug. "This place is so fancy. Dotty does not mess around," Willow said, walking into Lana's room. Lana scanned the hallway, but Jane was nowhere to be seen. She closed the door and followed her friend inside.

"Where's your wife?"

"She wants to take a short nap before the tour starts. Jane has been working so hard, and her motion sickness takes a lot out of her. She needs some time to decompress. What do you say, should we hit the streets and check this place out?"

"That sounds great." Lana had hoped to get a few minutes here and there with her friend, but knew that she was technically on call the entire duration of the trip. And Willow was in Paris to enjoy a romantic vacation with her partner. It wasn't as if they were on a girls' trip together.

Lana dumped her winter jacket onto her bed and pulled out a windbreaker.

It was slightly warmer than back home, but much drier and sunnier, which made a world of difference.

They wandered aimlessly along the River Seine, admiring the incredible architecture lining both sides, as well as the many boats chugging up and down its slow-moving water. Along the waterfront were young people picnicking with their friends and artists selling sketches of local sites. Others were creating caricatures of tourists or playing guitars, busking for money. Lana danced in time with the Bob Dylan tune a long-haired young man was strumming. As they walked along two Parisians locked in a passionate embrace, Willow asked, "So have you had any luck with the Seattle Singles yet?"

"Not really," Lana fibbed, still unwilling to share more about her budding relationship just yet. Willow was her best friend, but she needed time to find out whether Chad was a good match for her, without any external pressure. "If I get serious with anyone, I'll bring him by for your approval."

"You'd better," Willow said, her expression strict before she broke into laughter.

Soon, a need for caffeine led them to a café's terrace. The sun warmed their bodies as they drank lattes from dainty cups and watched the world go by.

"Oh my, Paris is even more beautiful than I expected," Lana said, glad to sit for a minute. The city blocks here were comparable to four back home. Everything was so spread apart. As much as she wanted to try out the Metro, she did love walking the streets and feeling a part of the chaotic and busy Parisian life.

"And so much bigger!" Willow exclaimed, stretching out her calves and ankles. "It feels good to move around after that flight. Eleven hours is a long time to be cooped up. You seemed so at ease; I'm impressed you don't mind it more."

"It is a job requirement," Lana teased. "Say, about that flight." She stirred her coffee, unable to look Willow in the eye. "Are you and Jane going to be okay? The trip's not even begun, and you are already at each other's throats."

"After being together for seven years, I thought I knew her better. I underestimated her dedication to her patients, and our fighting in the plane was her way of letting me know that she is not happy."

"Yeah, that's pretty obvious. I know I haven't been there for you enough since I started this job." Lana put a hand on Willow's, locking eyes with her. "And I am truly sorry about that. But what exactly are you fighting about? What's preventing you from starting the IVF treatment?"

"Jane wants me to sell my yoga studio because she doesn't want to cut back on her hours. Which is ridiculous. If we are going to have a family together, she can't be on call seven days a week. Whenever I ask when she is going to hire a second doctor to help share the load, she gets mad at me and clams up. It's like she refuses to accept that she can't have it all."

"Seven days a week? Geez, I knew she was working a lot of overtime, but I didn't realize she was doing it all herself."

"This wasn't how it was supposed to go. She told me she would hire at least one more doctor once she had enough patients to make her practice profitable. But now that she's in that position, she refuses to even consider one. It's not like she can't find a suitable candidate. Several of her doctor friends have made it clear that they would gladly work with her, but she won't even consider it. My yoga studio might not be as profitable as her practice, but I've worked my butt off to get it up and running. Now that we are finally in the black, she wants me to sell it off! It's not fair."

Lana took a long sip of her coffee, not wanting to take a side.

"Last week I said I would make the IVF appointment if she signed a baby-prenup, but Jane laughed me out of the room," Willow admitted. "She said if I can't trust her to be true to her word, then we shouldn't be having a baby together."

"Oh, Willow, I wish I knew what to say. Babies are something Ron and I never got around to." Lana paused for a moment to choose her words carefully. "I hate to ask, but there are four other couples on the tour. Are you going to be able to be civil to each other?"

"Of course! She's made it clear where she stands, so now it's my turn to react. And I'm choosing not to. Besides, the motion sickness didn't help. Those belladonna drops took the edge off, but didn't suppress it completely.

Once she's had a nap, Jane will feel better, and the evening will go more smoothly. I promise."

Lana hesitated before nodding. She did love Jane, but also knew that the woman was stubborn with a capital S. Once she got something in her mind, it was difficult for her to let it go. But in this case, Lana had no choice but to trust that Willow was right. "Great. Well, that's settled. Do you mind if we go back to the hotel? I could use a short nap before our group meets up in the lobby."

"Sounds good to me, I think I'll do the same. Jet lag does take a lot of out you," Willow agreed. "How do we pay the bill? Do you see our waiter?"

"I haven't seen him since we ordered these."

"I'll go inside and pay," Willow offered.

"No, wait," Lana said as she raised her arm like they did in movies and shouted, "*Garçon!*" She smiled mischievously. "I've always wanted to do that."

6

What Was I To You?

Lana skipped down the carpeted steps to the hotel's grand lobby. Randy was a few steps behind. He'd overdone it climbing this afternoon and his leg was throbbing, slowing his pace. Lana ran her hand over the cool marble railing, wishing Chad was here with her, when a distinguished-looking gentleman standing in the lobby turned around, as if he was searching for someone. It was Chad! Lana froze and blinked repeatedly, certain her eyes were deceiving her. She hadn't just conjured up her boyfriend, had she?

Lana rushed over and hugged him tight. "You're real! How did you know I was here?"

Chad pushed out of her embrace, his eyes widening in shock. "What are you doing here?" he hissed.

Lana frowned at him. "What do you mean? Aren't you here to see me?"

"I'm here on vacation with my wife, Miranda."

Lana squeezed her eyes tight. "Oh no, not again," she whimpered. When she looked up at Chad, tears were forming in her eyes. "Who are you?"

He took her by the hand and pulled her into a corner of the vast lobby. "My name is Chad, but I'm not single, nor am I a website developer. I am here with my wife and her friends."

Lana couldn't believe her bad luck. Her new boyfriend and his wife were staying at the same hotel as her group. Could this week get any worse? She choked back a sob. "What was I to you?"

"A bit of fun. Unfortunately we never did get to play around…"

Lana slapped his cheek. "How dare you!"

Chad glared at her. "We barely know each other. It shouldn't be difficult pretending to be strangers. Why are you in Paris, anyway? I thought you were in Japan."

"I guess we are both liars. I don't work at the travel agency, I work for them as a guide. I'm here to lead a group for a week."

Chad's face drained of color as he whimpered, "Oh, no."

"Chad, what is going on?" a woman called out. Lana turned to her. She was a beautiful, elegantly dressed woman in her late fifties. Her stern expression softened when she saw Lana's name tag.

"Oh, you must be from Wanderlust Tours. I'm Miranda, and this is Chad. We're one of the three couples that booked together."

Lana gulped. Chad wasn't just staying in the same hotel, he was part of her group. Her week could apparently get much worse. Thoughts of their kisses filled her with shame. She was the other woman, albeit unknowingly. Lana was grateful that they had gone out only a few times and never been intimate. That would have made this week impossible.

Lana plastered on her official smile and held out her hand. "It's lovely to meet you, Miranda and Chad," Lana said graciously, keeping her eyes focused on Chad's wife.

Randy walked over to them, his puzzled expression indicating that he didn't know what to do next. "Randy, this is Miranda and Chad, two of our guests. We were just about to join you."

"Great, hello, it's good to meet you both. It looks like we are ready to go. Everyone is by the entrance." He pointed towards a cluster of middle-aged couples. "Is there a shuttle bus, or are we supposed to call a cab?" Randy asked.

Miranda and Chad stared at him as if he was insane. "Aren't you one of our guides?" Chad asked.

"No, I am, but I'm in training. Lana is the lead on this trip," he said. Chad rolled his eyes and led his wife towards their friends.

"Sorry about that," Randy muttered once they'd walked off. "I should have pulled you apart to ask."

"Don't worry about it. But yes, next time, just take me aside. The guests do pay quite a bit for the trip, and I don't want them to feel as if they are getting shorted somehow."

Randy hung his head in shame.

"Randy, it's not that big a deal! The tour doesn't officially start until we are on the boat," she joked.

He chuckled in acknowledgement. "I'll keep my mouth shut and follow your lead."

Lana started to correct him, then thought better of it. "Okay, are you ready to get this tour started?"

Randy's eyes shone. "Yes, ma'am!"

Lana turned to walk to their guests, but Randy stayed put. "Ah, Lana, there is one more thing I want to ask before we join the others."

Lana stepped back, puzzled.

Randy's face turned bright red as he looked to the ground. "I couldn't help but notice you and Chad talking. And you, ah, seem to know each other quite well. Is there anything I should know about, seeing how his wife is on our tour, too?"

Lana sighed in frustration. "I recently started online dating, and unfortunately, Chad was the first to respond. I had no idea he was married."

Randy looked towards Chad and Miranda, a few feet away, laughing and joking around with their friends. "That's a pretty crappy way of finding out."

Lana snorted. "You could say that. Luckily, we only went out a few times and nothing happened. As far as I'm concerned, we're complete strangers."

"Are you certain you will be able to make it through the week, with him on our tour?"

"Of course! I'm a professional. Though if you could look after Chad, I would be quite grateful."

Randy puffed up his chest, reminding Lana of a big brother about to beat up his little brother's bully. "No problem, Lana, I've got this."

Lana laid a hand on his arm. "Thanks, Randy. Now why don't we go introduce ourselves to the other guests?"

7

Cruising the River Seine

Lana's guests dutifully filed into the sleek riverboat, large enough to comfortably seat twenty. The interior was mahogany; the cushions, covered in deep blue suede. Tables for four lined each side. At the back, several had been pushed together to form one long table enough to seat six. The group of three couples migrated to the largest, the wives clustered together at one end, away from the husbands.

That's odd for a romantic cruise, Lana thought. She and her ex-husband had been together nine years, but she had never tired of sitting by his side. He had been her best friend and confidante for so long, it was still strange not to be able to talk to him about her new adventures as a tour guide. But their break had been sudden and definite; there was no reason for them to keep in contact.

Lana looked again at the three couples. She would never be able to forget Miranda, but didn't quite have the other two wives, Tamara and Sabine, down yet. The women were obviously good friends, already laughing and exchanging gossip about mutual acquaintances back home. Their husbands, Edward, Chad, and Henry, however, didn't appear to know each other that well. Their body language and stilted conversation told her that they didn't meet up as regularly as their wives did.

Willow and Jane sat at a table on the left; Angie and Bernie, the fourth couple to book this trip, took a table on the right. Both were dressed in loose-fitting clothing that looked to be made from natural fibers. Lana glanced at their feet, expecting to see Birkenstocks. She was not disappointed. Angie had a large black amulet around her neck and rings on each finger. Her husband also had a thick silver chain around his neck, though his turquoise stone was significantly smaller than that of his wife. His long wavy hair, streaked with white, almost reached his shoulders.

Two more empty tables were set for dinner service. Randy laid his bag and map down on the one just behind Willow and Jane. Lana began walking over to join him when Willow cleared her throat and patted the chair next to her. Lana raised an eyebrow, surprised her friend would want company during the first romantic dinner in Paris. She hoped it wasn't because Willow wanted her to play referee.

"Hey, Willow. It is customary for the guides to sit separately, so we can help other clients without disturbing your meal, as well as talk through any issues one of us may be having," Lana explained.

"Of course, you are on duty now."

Lana's smile faltered, unsure whether her friend meant to sound snide or was just under too much stress. Either way, she ignored it, saying, "Thanks for understanding. Enjoy your dinner, okay?" Lana and Willow both looked to Jane, but she kept her gaze focused on the river.

Lana hoped Jane would give Willow a break soon so they could actually enjoy their week. They hadn't been on vacation together in several years and probably wouldn't get the chance to do so again for quite some time.

Lana took the chair across from Randy and pulled the revised itinerary out of her bag.

"Is this our table, Lana? I wasn't sure if we were supposed to sit here or stand with the crew."

"We are allowed to sit here and have the same dinner as the guests. It's just, if they have questions, answering them is more of priority than savoring our meal," she said with a smile, hoping Randy would feel more confident soon.

Randy chuckled and leaned back. "I gotcha. Is there anything we should do before dinner is served?"

"Yes, there is. Dotty mailed me another revision to our itinerary. I've printed off a copy for everyone, including you. I think it's best to hand them out now, instead of waiting until later. I wouldn't be surprised if some guests have questions about the changes," Lana said, giggling as she handed him a sheet of paper.

Randy tilted his head as his brows furrowed.

"You'll have to read it and see what you think."

"You do have my curiosity piqued," he said and began scanning the additional information. As he reached Valentine's Day, he began to laugh. "You have got to be joking—did a guest really request that?"

"Yep. I have a feeling not everyone will want to join in. We'll see what happens. Would you mind handing these out while I give the introduction spiel? It's probably better to do that now, before the waiters bring out the appetizers."

Lana stood and cleared her throat, standing in the middle of the dining area so that everyone could hear her. "Ladies and gentlemen, it is a pleasure to welcome you to Paris. We at Wanderlust Tours hope you enjoy your stay in this lovely city and the day trips we have planned."

Lana looked around at her clients, making eye contact with them all. "We will be embarking soon and sailing along the River Seine while we dine. Before dinner is served, I do want to inform you of three tours we have added to the schedule. Randy is passing out a new itinerary. As you can see, some of the planned free afternoons and evenings have been filled in. No one is required to go on any of these additional trips. We wanted to book them ahead of time, to ensure that everyone has the chance to participate, if they wish. I'll come by your table in case you have questions about these updates or Paris in general. This is your trip—make the most of it!"

Lana grabbed ahold of the table as the boat began moving away from the river's edge. Moments later, a waiter came around and offered them all a glass of champagne. Lana clinked glasses with Randy then took a tentative sip. It smelled sweet, and the bubbles tickled her nose. "Oh, yum. It's drier than I'd expected, but quite delicious," Lana said, drinking her glass too quickly. Here she was, enjoying her first glass of real champagne, and in Paris to boot! She wasn't certain whether it was the sudden burst of alcohol flowing through her veins or simply the fact that they'd now gotten the tour underway, but she felt as if this was going to be a great trip, despite Chad's presence on it.

Soon they were passing the Notre Dame Cathedral, staring up at the gothic towers gracing each side. The famous flying buttresses, meant to hold up the roof, looked so forlorn. The main cathedral, still visibly damaged by the devastating fires of 2019, remained magnificent nevertheless. It was wonderful to be so low on the water, looking up at these historic monuments, especially as twilight set in. Most were dramatically illuminated by both the sun's last rays and hundreds of tiny light bulbs.

After she and Randy finished their champagne, Lana said, "The guests have had a chance to read the revised itinerary. I think we'd better go around and see if there are any questions or concerns. If someone does not wish to join one of the day tours, Dotty likes us to help them arrange an alternative—if the guest wants our help, that is," she added quickly, knowing that Randy was quite eager and would be perhaps too willing to offer alternative suggestions. Lana knew it was cheaper for Dotty to stick to the planned itinerary.

Lana started with the longest table, hoping Chad would stay true to his word and pretend not to know her. So far so good; Chad ignored her approach, instead taking tiny sips of his champagne, then jotting down notes on a small pad next to this plate.

Lana smiled broadly as she moved toward the wives and Randy stood across from the men. "Hello again, Henry, Sabine, Edward, Tamara, Miranda, and Chad. Does anyone have any questions about the day trips? Randy and I are happy to answer them."

"I have a question," Miranda said, as she tapped on the itinerary with a manicured nail. "Is this a misprint? Are we really booked to see a show at the Moulin Rouge on Valentine's Day?"

Lana tried to keep her smile plastered on. "It's not a mistake. We had a request to see the show, and this was the only day they had tickets available."

"I bet. What pervert wants to see that kind of show on Valentine's Day?"

"Honestly, I don't know who requested it," Lana explained patiently. "All I know is that it was approved by my manager and booked the next day. If anyone does not want to join us at the Moulin Rouge, I can reserve a table for you at a number of romantic restaurants in the city center."

"I think the show sounds like fun," Tamara said.

Miranda's eyebrows knitted together. "Wait, did you request this to get back at me for the baguette workshop? I told you before, I don't like macarons. Why would I want to learn to make them? And baguettes are the symbol of France and we are in Paris. Besides, I need to know how to shape them properly. Mine always end up malformed."

"No, I didn't suggest the Moulin Rouge, though I wish I had. I bet someone wanted to surprise me," Tamara said, and bumped her husband's arm to get his attention.

"What?" Edward asked, looking up from his smartphone in irritation.

Tamara rolled her eyes. "Can't you put that thing away? We're on vacation."

"The stock market doesn't take a vacation. Why should I?"

"So you can enjoy Paris. We never go away anymore."

Edward snorted. "Without our stock portfolio, we wouldn't be able to afford this trip. You should be more grateful," he said dismissively, turning away from his wife.

Tamara sucked up her breath as if she was readying for an attack, then released it, choosing to turn back to her friends instead. "You wanted to see the real Paris, Miranda. I bet the Moulin Rouge show is going to be a riot. We had a blast in Vegas, right?"

"Yeah, the Chippendales show was great, but this is burlesque. I doubt they'll have much for us to ogle," Miranda said.

Sabine laughed. "You're right. That was a pretty incredible show. Honestly, I don't care what we do. I'm just glad to be with you two," she said, grabbing Miranda's and Tamara's hands. "And our husbands, of course," she added, clearly as an afterthought.

Her husband, Henry, used the opportunity to kiss his wife on the cheek, saying, "That's the Musée d'Orsay. Isn't it beautiful?" So far, he was the only one of the six actually looking out the windows, watching Paris float by.

Sabine gazed outside, and her face lit up. "Look at those swans. I can't believe how big they are."

"Hi, I just wanted to pop over and introduce myself before dinner arrives,"

Angie said, addressing the group. She pushed her way around Lana so she could get closer to the large group.

"It sure is great to meet you all. I'm Angie, and that's my husband, Bernie." Bernie waved from their table. "We just moved to Seattle from Florida and thought this would be a great way to meet other Seattleites. I have to say, your auras are so vibrant, it's like a rainbow surrounding your table."

"Oh no, a healy feelie," Edward groaned.

Angie ignored him and pulled out a handful of pink stones. "I'm opening a healing crystals shop on Capitol Hill next month. Seeing how it is Valentine's week, I wanted to share some of my rose quartz with you. It's also known as the love stone," Angie added with a wink. "They are quite rare."

She handed six stones to Miranda, so that she could pass them around the table. "I brought one for each of you. Their energetic vibrations positively affect our physical and emotional well-being. I sleep with them under my pillow. I have the most vivid dreams, yet feel so rested when I wake up."

Miranda frowned at her stone, but did hand the other five to Sabine, sitting on her right.

"Wow, I've never seen anything this high quality before," Sabine said as she held her stone up to the light. "It's beautiful."

"Let me see those," Tamara said, snatching the four remaining rocks out of her hand. "Geez, these look expensive."

"Oh, they are, trust me, but not unreasonably so. I sell the crystals individually and as part of my healing jewelry line. Our website is already online." Angie leaned over and held out her ring-covered hand for Sabine to see. "No children were exploited when mining our silver, I guarantee it."

Is Angie actually selling her jewelry to my clients? Lana thought. She didn't know what to do. It didn't feel right having a passenger peddling their products to the others. Yet, Sabine did appear to be genuinely interested.

"It's important to know where the metals and crystals come from. There's so much information online these days and so many watchdog organizations. You are doing the right thing," Sabine said.

"I don't believe in that new-age stuff. You can have mine back," Miranda said, her voice filled with disdain.

Tamara snatched it out of her hand. "I'll have yours, then. Not all of our families are stinking rich. How much does one of these go for, anyway?"

Lana walked away from Angie's sales pitch, choosing to check in with Willow and Jane instead.

8

Love Stones

"Hello, ladies, are you enjoying the ride so far?"

A team of waiters had just served their appetizer—a large plate filled with a pâté-like substance and a sprig of onion. Lana grabbed hers and sat down next to Willow. Randy looked so forlorn on his own, but Lana wanted to first see whether Willow and Jane were getting along.

Turns out, she made the right decision. As soon as her backside hit the chair, Jane pointed to the itinerary. "I thought we were going to have more time to explore the city on our own."

"Yes, well, the extra requests all required reservations, so we scheduled them during the group's free time. If you don't want to attend the baking workshop, horticulture tour, or Moulin Rouge show, you don't have to do. That's the beauty of a Wanderlust tour—you get to pick and choose."

"I don't know about the workshop or plants tour, but the Moulin Rouge might be entertaining, Jane," Willow said. "It's definitely something different and very French."

"I'm not really in the mood to watch women degrade themselves," Jane snapped.

"You're not in the mood to do much of anything, are you?" Willow countered.

Lana rose, her plate in hand. *So much for their truce*, she thought. "Dotty did send along a list of romantic restaurants. I can book you into one, if you would rather skip the Moulin Rouge show. I'll leave you to discuss it," Lana said, keeping her tone neutral. "If you will excuse me, I just remembered that I have to explain a few things to Randy before we dock. Enjoy your meal, ladies." The last thing she wanted to do was listen to her friends fight on their first night in Paris.

Lana set her plate down across from Randy. "How are you doing?"

"Pretty good," he answered, though his eyes were wide with anxiety and he seemed to be shaking a little.

She smiled at him. "Try to relax. We're here to help each other out. I'll worry about the guests tonight. Why don't you just be a fly on the wall and see how I handle their concerns."

Randy's pulse must have normalized because the color returned to his face. "That would be great. Thanks, Lana."

"Don't worry about it." She looked again at her plate. "What the heck is this?" she muttered, glancing at the menu.

"*Foie gras*. That's pâté made from the goose liver," Randy answered before she could find it on the menu.

"Oh la la. I knew *foie gras* was a French delicacy, but I'd never seen it before. It's not what I was expecting. What do you think of it?" Lana asked, looking at his portion. "You must like it because your plate is clean."

Randy winced. "It's not something I would order again, but it was worth trying once. I hate leaving food on my plate. My grandma used to yell at us kids when we would leave a bite behind. She grew up during the Great Depression, and it affected how she regarded food. Even mold wouldn't stop her, I'm afraid."

"You're not really selling it, but I'm going to try it anyway." Lana took a bite of her appetizer and almost gagged. *Foie gras* was something she had always wanted to try, but now that it was in her mouth, she was certain that it was not her cup of tea. She swigged back a glass of sparkling water to wash away the taste just as Angie took her place across from her husband.

"How did it go?" Bernie asked.

"Alright. I think they're more lookie-loos than buyers."

"Oh well, you gave it a shot."

Lana shook her head slightly, wondering whether Angie was going to try selling her and Randy crystals next.

Angie finished her appetizer in four bites then looked around for more. "I'm starving." She picked up the menu and held it far away from her face, frowning. "Darn it, I forgot my glasses, and the letters are just too small. What are we eating tonight?"

"I swear, if your head wasn't attached, you would probably lose that, too!" Bernie laughed as he picked up the menu. "Let's see, tonight we are dining on salmon filet with a lobster bisque and crispy vegetables."

When Angie grunted in response and glanced around, Lana figured this was as good a time as any to ask them about the extra tours.

"I hope dinner sounds good to you," Lana said as she approached their table.

"It sounds fine, though more of an experience than a belly filler. I haven't eaten anything since the plane ride over and could eat a horse right about now."

Lana chuckled. "I can always ask if there's enough for you to have seconds."

Angie waved her offer away. "What can we do for you, kiddo?"

Lana couldn't help but furrow her eyebrows. Maybe "kiddo" was an East Coast thing. "I wanted to see if you had any questions about the revised itinerary."

"That's nice of you," Bernie said in his nasal voice. "I was glad to see the baking workshop; that sounds like fun. Though I don't know if we'll join you for the horticulture tour; that doesn't interest me."

"No? Oh, I was looking forward to seeing it," Angie said. "Did you know the garden was where Louis XIII's doctor grew the medicinal plants he used to treat the king? That sounds fascinating to me."

Bernie nodded appreciatively. "You got me there, babe. If you want to go, I'm in. Lana, we'll tag along on that one, too."

Angie took his hands and kissed his fingertips. "That's my Bernie—opening himself up to new experiences."

They leaned over the table and met in the middle, rubbing noses together before sitting down again.

"Oh, brother," Lana muttered under her breath and she returned to Randy.

When the main course didn't show up immediately, Angie decided to introduce herself to Willow and Jane, as well.

Lana sucked in her breath, hoping for the best. All they needed was for Jane to tear into Angie on their first night in Paris. She leaned forward and put one finger over her lips so that Randy knew to stay quiet. She wanted to keep tabs on their conversation in case she needed to jump in.

"Hello, again," Angie said as she approached Willow and Jane's table. "I don't want to interrupt, but I brought everyone a present. It's rose quartz, to celebrate Valentine's Day."

"Love stones," Willow said, bringing out the most radiant smile on Angie's face.

"Exactly. Not only do they nurture love, they positively affect our emotional well-being. Please, these are for you."

"I'm a doctor. I don't believe in reading auras or treating symptoms with stones," Jane said dismissively.

Lana was surprised by Jane's bluntness, but then she did look exhausted. And a two-hour cruise after an eleven-hour flight must be a sort of torture for someone with extreme motion sickness.

"But you do take herbal treatments," Willow said evenly. "Don't mind my wife; she suffers from motion sickness." Jane looked out the window instead of responding.

"Ooh, are you married? That's wonderful! Everyone should be able to be with whoever they want to be with. Don't you agree?"

Willow cocked her head. "Yes, I do."

"I do have some citrine crystal back in my hotel room. It helps alleviate nausea."

"That's really kind of you, thanks," Willow said. Jane raised an eyebrow yet remained silent.

The waiters soon returned, serving their main course.

"I better let you enjoy your meal," Angie said. "I'll give you the citrine the next time I see you."

"Great, we appreciate it," Willow said.

After Angie returned to her table, Willow turned to Jane, concern in her voice. "Did you take your belladonna?"

"When we were in the hotel room. I don't want to take more and overdo it." Jane noticed Lana listening in. "We'll be heading back to shore soon, right, Lana?"

"Yes, and then you can rest for the night. We don't have any more cruises planned. Just a few bus rides, but judging by the terrible traffic, I doubt we'll go fast enough for you to feel sick again."

"That sounds good." The relief in her voice was evident. Jane looked out across the water and gazed up at the Eiffel Tower, standing so regally in the center of a large park. "I can't believe we are actually in Paris," she murmured. "I can't remember the last time we took a vacation."

"Four years and three months ago," Willow said.

"Was it so long ago? That's not good." Jane took Willow's hand. "I'm sorry I snapped at you. I think I need to be land bound for a while. My stomach won't stop doing somersaults."

"I think you're right." Willow smiled gently, then looked away. "I'm sorry I didn't ask you first. I thought it would be so romantic to surprise you with a week away. But I didn't think about your patients."

"If you had asked, I would have said no. And after all these long months of overtime, I think a break will do me good." Jane gazed back outside. "It's too bad I can't take being on boats or planes for long. It is such a beautiful view."

"Yes, it is," Willow said, her eyes on Jane.

Internally Lana was cheering; there was hope for her friends' relationship yet.

9

Bad Vibes

Lana was deep into dreamland when a harsh ringing shattered her peaceful sleep. It was the hotel phone on her night table. *It's only our first night and already the guests are antsy*, Lana thought. She sat up with a huff, wishing she dared let Randy take a turn on night duty during this trip. Normally the guides shared the responsibility of dealing with any problems or troublesome situations that arose in the night. Since beginning her job, she was amazed at how often a guest had a problem immediately after she had crawled into bed.

She took a quick swig of water, then answered the phone, her tone as professional as possible. "This is Lana, how can I help you?"

"Lana! Thank goodness! The receptionist keeps connecting me to the wrong room. I don't think she understands my French."

"What is it, Angie? Is something wrong?" Lana was suddenly alert. Angie sounded distraught.

"Can you come to room 11? We've got a problem."

"Of course. I'll be right there." Lana pulled on the same clothes she had just shed and scurried down the hall to her guests' room, all the time wondering what crisis would warrant being roused out of bed at midnight.

Before Lana's knuckles could connect with room 11's door, it flew open. Angie stood inside, wrapped up in a thick bathrobe, her short, spiky hair standing on end. She looked quite anxious. Her husband sat on the edge of the bed, head in his hands, their packed bags at his feet.

"What is going on? Were you robbed?" Lana glanced around at the windows and balcony. The glass appeared to be intact.

"I simply cannot sleep in this room. The energy is far too negative. Can't you feel it?"

Lana's surge of adrenaline rushed out of her body, leaving her feeling deflated. "What?"

"I tried moving the furniture around so it had better feng shui, but I think the readjustment will need more time to take effect."

"Would you be willing to give it seven more hours? If you still feel strange vibes in the morning, I can arrange for you to be moved to a new room."

Angie shook her head fervently. "No way. I simply cannot sleep in here, Lana. If I don't get at least six hours of deep slumber, I won't be able to function tomorrow," Angie said, her voice trembling.

Lana closed her eyes and took a deep cleansing breath, hoping this was some sort of ultra-realistic nightmare. When she opened them, Angie was standing before her, a pleading look on her face.

Lana took in the extravagantly decorated room. It looked exactly like hers, right down to the identical nightstands and art deco table lamps. The only difference was the hum of traffic. When she looked out the window, a truck roared past a minivan on the busy street below, beeping in protest as it swerved around the smaller vehicle. Lana wondered whether the noise had anything to do with the bad vibes Angie was feeling.

Realizing her guests' happiness was her top priority, she pushed down her snarky thoughts and nodded diplomatically. "I am not as sensitive to the energy as you are, but if you want to be moved to another room, I will be happy to ask the receptionist if there is another one available."

Angie clapped her hands together. "Bless you, Lana. Nothing would be worse than spending a week in a room that gives you the chills."

"Let me go see what they have available. I'll call up to your room when I know more, okay?" Lana walked swiftly down to the lobby, hoping to find quick resolution to this matter so she could get some sleep. Tomorrow was going to be a long day of walking tours, and she was paid to be bright and cheerful. A good night's sleep made her job so much easier.

Unfortunately their hotel was booked out, meaning there was no room to switch to. There was only one other option available.

Angie answered on the first ring. "Yes?"

"There are no other rooms available, so I have arranged for us to change rooms. New sheets are being sent up now. Give me ten minutes to pack up my bags, then I'll come over and we can switch."

"Excellent. Thanks, Lana."

Luckily Lana traveled so lightly it only took a few minutes to repack her belongings. When she knocked on room 11, Angie and Bernie were standing by the door, ready to go. "I just put the new sheets on the bed," Angie said. "We sure do appreciate this, Lana." Bernie stayed silent, allowing his wife to pull the strings. Lana wondered whether he, too, felt the negative energy, or whether he just wanted to make his wife happy so he could get a good night's sleep. Bernie nodded as he passed, a sheepish grin on his face.

"No problem, I hope you can sleep in that room."

"I'm certain we will. Good night."

Lana dropped her luggage by the door and sprung onto the bed, still clothed. Her eyes drooped closed automatically. She forced herself to sit up and undress, knowing she would sleep better for it. Lana used the nightstand to push herself up, knocking a small book off in the process. Lana picked it up and turned it over. It was a small album of photos, with a close-up of Bernie and Angie on the cover. Curious, Lana opened it. Inside were forty or so photographs of them. It began with Bernie feeding Angie cake at their wedding, and spanned several decades of married life. A smile tugged on her lips as she gazed at the happy couple, who were always making silly faces and posing together with friends. Almost all of the pictures were taken in exotic locations. *They obviously love to travel*, Lana thought, curious to see where exactly they had been.

Captivated by the locations they had visited, Lana had reached the end of the album before she noticed their clothing. With the exception of the last two shots, they were dressed in expensive designer clothes and lots of gold jewelry in all of them. There was not a single photo of them in the flowing robes, tie-dyed T-shirts, and chunky jewelry that they wore on this trip. Based on these photos, both appeared to be business investors, not new-agers. *Why are they pretending to be hippies?* Lana wondered.

A knock on the door made her jump. She sprung up and looked through the peephole. It was Angie. Embarrassed at having snuck a look at their private photos, she quickly put the album back where she'd found it, before answering the door.

"I'm so sorry to bother you again, but I think I left something behind. Do you mind if I take a look?" Angie asked. She seemed nervous.

"Sure, come on in," Lana said, as brightly as her sleep deprivation would allow.

"There it is!" Angie cried, her relief evident. She turned to Lana, the photo album in both hands. "I gave this to my husband last week and would have hated to lose it so soon."

"Oh, what is it?" Lana asked innocently.

"Photos from our thirty-one years of marriage. We just celebrated our anniversary, and I made him this present as a surprise."

"That's really sweet of you," Lana said, smiling genuinely.

Angie tucked the mini-album into an oversized pocket, which itself disappeared into the generous folds of her peasant dress. She turned to leave, then whipped back around again and took Lana's hands. "The energy in your room is magical. Thank you so much for switching with us."

She pulled a flat black stone out of her other pocket. "I have an amulet for you, to help improve the sphere in here. This is tourmaline; it dissolves negative energy." Angie pressed it into Lana's hand. "I wanted to burn some sage to purify the room, but my husband was afraid it would set off the fire alarms. If you want to try it tomorrow with the windows open, I'm game."

"No thanks. I am not as attuned to the room's energy as you are. I think I'll be fine."

"Bless you, child." Angie grabbed her arm and squeezed. "I appreciate you understanding."

"I'll see you at breakfast."

10

Jardin des Tuileries

February 13—Day Two of the Wanderlust Tour in Paris, France

Lana gazed at the paintings before her, trying to figure out why the water lilies touched her soul. Standing in the center of the oval hall, its curved walls covered with Claude Monet's massive masterpieces, Lana felt as if she was in the middle of a vast pond surrounded by the glorious flowers floating on its surface. It was magical.

"Did he use chalk? Or is it paint? In this low light, the water appears to shimmer. I've never seen anything like it," Tamara whispered to Sabine. Lana was glad to see they were just as in awe of Monet's work as she was.

Lana stepped close to one of the *Nymphéas* paintings, captivated by his rendering of the flowers, when she felt her phone vibrate in her pocket, reminding her they needed to get moving on to the next stop of the day.

This afternoon's destinations were so close to each other, Dotty had not hired a local guide for this portion of the day. After twisting and turning her way around Montmartre this morning, luckily with an experienced local guide, Lana had been skeptical. However, when she looked at a map, she realized it would be a cinch to get her guests from the Musée Orangerie, where they currently were, to the Louvre Museum. Both monumental institutions were located on opposite sides of the Jardin des Tuileries, a public park in the heart of Paris. Local guides were booked for each museum;

all Lana had to do was walk her guests from one end of the park to the other. Easy as pie.

Their guide at the Musée Orangerie had finished up early, allowing them a few minutes to digest Monet's masterpieces in silence. Not wanting to disturb the meditative silence pervading the exhibition space, Lana walked up to each guest and quietly asked them to accompany her upstairs. Her group would have an hour to lunch in one of the many cafés dotted around the Jardin des Tuileries before the Louvre tour began.

Once they had reassembled outside, Lana led her group down a staircase and into the Tuileries Gardens. The thick clusters of trees lining both sides of the path were manicured flat, forming a large green box on either side. Lana had never seen anything like it. The plants seemed to defy nature. She was so used to the rough, old-growth forests in Olympic National Park and loved the randomness of nature. Yet here in this formal French garden, symmetry dominated. It was strangely beautiful, Lana thought, just different than back home. Oddly enough, the gravelly paths were dusty, in spite of last night's rainstorm. Within minutes, her shoes were soon covered in a light gray powder.

As they casually strolled past statues, grassy patches, and flower beds, Lana watched the plethora of hip Parisians out walking their dogs. *Dotty would love it here*, she thought. Almost all of the pooches on leashes were wearing colorful sweaters or body warmers. As one particularly snooty older woman walked past, Lana realized her dog was wearing the same haute couture as its owner. "I didn't know they made Chanel for dogs," Lana mumbled, pulling out her phone and snapping a photo for Dotty.

As she rushed to catch back up to her group, Lana unbuttoned her jacket, relishing the warming temperatures. It was a gorgeous and crisp spring day, warmer than in Seattle and certainly sunnier. Lana was glad to leave the soft spray of winter rain behind. She always missed the sun in the wintertime.

Lana was pleased to see how well her guests were getting along this morning. They all seemed happier and more relaxed now that they were out and about. Paris was magical in that way. She couldn't wait to come back here with her lover one day. Chad may have fooled her, but at least they hadn't dated long or slept together. Considering they had both lied about who they were, it was easy to forget her feelings for him.

To Lana's relief, Chad did his best to ignore and avoid her. His wife seemed nice enough, though quite distant and cool. Lana only hoped that Miranda never found out how close they had gotten or how they had met. Lana would die from the shame, she imagined.

The three friend-couples did tend to stick together, meaning Angie and Bernie and her friends Willow and Jane gravitated towards each other. Lana was glad to hear Jane apologize to Angie about her behavior on the boat. The older woman wrapped her up in an all-forgiving hug, and that was that.

Angie had slept so well, she couldn't stop talking about how generous and kind Lana was, which was sweet. However, her raving about having tea on the balcony and enjoying this morning's sunrise over the Eiffel Tower did make Lana wonder how much the energy of the room had to do with their wanting to move. The traffic underneath room 11 wasn't horrible, but it was constant. And the views were nothing to write home about.

Randy rushed around from one couple to the next, checking in to make sure they were having a good time. Lana made a mental note to take him aside and ask him to tone it down. His zealousness was quite intense.

Walking at the front, hand in hand, were Willow and Jane. Lana was so glad they were being nice to each other today. If they couldn't rekindle their romance in one of the most romantic cities in the world, Lana didn't know what else they could do to make it happen.

All of a sudden, a red ball bounced onto the path and right into Jane's leg. She leaned down and picked it up as its owner, a small blonde child, waddled towards Jane. A toothless grin split her tiny face. Jane gently tossed the ball back and clapped as the girl caught it on the first try.

Lana felt hope in her heart. She and Willow were both so good with kids, they would make wonderful parents. They only had to find a way to get around this impasse. As the little girl ran back to her parents, Willow kissed Jane on the cheek before they resumed their stroll past the budding daffodils and boxy trees.

When her group reached the middle of the park, Lana checked her watch.

They only had forty minutes before their tour of the Louvre started. Lunch was going to have to be quick. "Okay, folks, the restaurant should be just ahead, on the left. Hopefully we can find enough seats on their terrace. This is a spectacular spring day." Lana hoped Dotty's information was up to date. Since it was her first time in Paris, she had to rely on her tour notes and guidebooks to fill in every detail.

As they walked farther into the park, Lana searched in vain for the café Dotty recommended.

"Would you look at that," Henry said while strolling arm in arm with his wife. They stopped to gaze at a concrete-enclosed pool on their right. Children were pushing wooden boats with long sticks, until the wind caught their raggedy sails and whisked them to the other side. Several little boys were racing their boats around the pond, laughing and screaming as they urged them on.

"Aren't those boats adorable?" Sabine said, hugging his arm tight.

Her group approached the water, watching the small watercraft in fascination. Next to the pond was a rickety handcart with more boats to rent. Right behind it was the Louvre, creating the perfect backdrop. Dotted around the pool were green metal chairs filled with locals and tourists soaking up the warm sunlight.

The men gravitated into a line, their arms crossing their torsos as they watched the children with envy.

Henry said, "I'd like to give it a go. What do you say? I bet I can sail mine around the pond first," he added jokingly.

"I'm willing to bet ten dollars that I win," Edward said, his tone serious.

"I was just kidding around," Henry said.

"Let's make it twenty," Bernie said, as he pulled out his wallet.

Chad handed a twenty-dollar bill to Edward. "I'm in."

Henry stared at the others but didn't reach for his money.

Randy must have noticed, too, because he sidled up to him. "I'm not much of a betting man, but I do want to try to sail one of those boats. I bet it's harder than it looks," he said. Henry grinned as they walked over to the boat rental cart. When they returned, wooden boats and sticks in hand, their grins and shy glances reminded Lana of two eager schoolboys.

"Lana, would you hold the pot?" Edward asked, sixty dollars in his hand.

Lana held her hands up. "I'd rather not get involved. Can your wife hold the money?"

Edward sauntered over to his wife, standing with her friends. "Can you hold onto this, babe?"

Tamara took the money and pulled him in for a long kiss. As they pulled apart, she slapped his backside and said, "Make me proud, tiger."

Edward stood up straighter, his chest puffed out as he walked to the cart and rented his boat.

As soon as their boats hit the water, the atmosphere intensified. The strong winds pulled the watercraft along at a clipped pace. The five middle-aged men trailing behind were all quickly out of breath.

In their struggle to be first, the three gamblers pushed and prodded their boats whenever they caught up to them, weaving between the French children playfully racing their watercraft around the pond. Randy's and Henry's boats trailed far behind.

Things got quickly out of hand once the men realized how hard it was to steer them. The short sticks were meant for kids, not adults, meaning the men had to squat down to use them effectively.

"The first one around wins," Edward shouted as his boat caught a gust of wind and shot around the bend. Chad raced to catch up, pushing his boat so hard, Lana was worried the stick would snap. Bernie slowed to a walk when his boat became stranded in the middle. As the other two zipped around the final bend, neck and neck, Edward sprinted forward, jabbing at his sails. Chad ran around him and sprung up onto the thin concrete ledge in an attempt to prod his own boat forward for the win.

"Hey, that's cheating!" Edward yelled as he sprung up to do the same, tripping on the concrete lip. His body's momentum drove him forward, smack into Chad. Both men fell into the water with a tremendous splash, spending ripples through the pond and toppling most of the wooden boats.

Cries from disappointed kids and curses from angry parents drew Lana to the water's edge. *What did those two buffoons do?* she thought.

Both men were locked in battle, Chad tugging on Edward's blazer as he tried to rise. "My phone is water resistant, not waterproof! Let me up!"

Randy sprung into the shallow pond and loosened Chad's grip. "Guys, come on! This is a game for kids, remember?"

Edward stalked out of the water, his phone already in his hand, oblivious to his wet clothes. Once the phone's start-up sounds chimed, Edward turned to Chad and smiled. "Looks like I won." Edward nodded to their boats. Chad's had submerged, but Edward's was still sailing, despite the rippling water.

Chad stormed out of the pool. A mob of angry parents encircled the two men. Lana pulled out several ten-euro notes from her cash supply, diplomatically distributing them to the affected parents. Only after she paid the vendor extra for their disruption to his boat rental service was her group free to go. She ushered them all to a patch of grass out of sight from the pond.

Lana glared at Edward and Chad. "I don't know what that was all about, but you can't go into the Louvre wet."

"I can take them back to the hotel to change," Randy offered. "My pants are wet, too."

"That would be great," she said, relief in her voice. Lana's excitement about being in Paris owed a lot to the Louvre. In college, she had taken Introduction to Art History, which she'd loved, and the teacher had urged all of her students to see the Louvre if they ever got the chance. While preparing for this tour, Lana had spent hours reading about the artwork inside. She knew it was enormous and impossible to view all of the art in one day, but she still wanted to see as much of it as possible. And in a few minutes, she would do just that. Lana looked towards the museum's glass pyramid entrance, only feet away, a smile playing on her lips.

"If you are fast, you should be able to catch the end of the tour," she added, before handing him five twenty-euro notes. "This should cover the ride and give you a little extra cash for incidental expenses."

Lana watched Randy, Chad, and Edward walk off to find a ride, hoping Randy was up to the task. So far, she had been appalled by his navigational skills. He tended to turn left when they should go right. Evidently it was easier for him to navigate around a mountain than a big urban city. Luckily, he wouldn't be alone.

11

So Much for Seeing the Louvre

After Randy left, Lana turned to the rest of her group. "We have enough time for a quick snack before the Louvre tour starts." She looked around for the nearest café and saw a food stall. "Anyone up for a crêpe?"

Minutes later, they were sitting in green chairs, turned to face the sun, while enjoying the delicately thin pancakes the French were known for. Lana's was filled with gooey chocolate and slices of strawberries. She'd discovered so many delicious new tastes and dishes since starting her job at Wanderlust Tours; it was definitely one of the perks of travel.

Lana was trying to recall the names of all the world-class art they were about to see when a stray dog caught her eye. It was one of many they had passed on their walks through the city. This one was bold enough to circle the chairs, searching for handouts.

"Oh, you poor thing. You look so hungry," Sabine cooed, patting her knee to beckon it closer.

"I would steer clear of the strays here," Jane counseled as Willow nodded in agreement. "You don't know what diseases they are carrying."

"I work with strays all the time, and my shots are up to date. Besides, this little guy is just hungry. He wouldn't hurt little old me," Sabine babbled as if she was talking to a child. She tore a piece of her crêpe off and threw it onto the ground. The dog came closer, its tail slowly wagging. Based on the many photos of her household pets Sabine had shown Lana at breakfast, it was pretty obvious that the woman was obsessed with animals of all kinds. Sabine tore off a bigger chunk and held it in her hands. The dog approached slowly and carefully took the food out of her hands.

"See, he's fine." Sabine set the remaining crêpe on her lap and reached out to pet the dog. It sniffed her fingertips tentatively, then clamped its jaw into her palm.

"Ow!" she screamed and rose, knocking the crêpe to the ground. The dog released his grip, grabbed her food, and ran off.

Lana couldn't believe their bad luck.

Jane jumped up to examine Sabine's hand. "It's bleeding profusely." She opened a new bottle of water and poured it over the wound. "Do you have a first-aid kit, Lana?"

"How could I be so foolish?" Sabine moaned.

"Don't worry, Sabine," Miranda said, holding her friend's shoulders close. "We know you love animals, but maybe you should leave the strays alone from now on."

Sabine nodded, teary-eyed.

"She's going to need antibiotics, a rabies booster, and maybe stitches. That dog really tore up her hand," Jane said.

Lana sighed in frustration as she handed Jane the emergency kit she always carried in her backpack. Randy was already halfway to the hotel by now. She had no choice but to accompany Sabine to the hospital. *So much for seeing the Louvre*, Lana thought.

12

Rabies Shots and Art History

After Lana got her increasingly smaller group to the Louvre and explained to their guide what had happened, she accompanied Sabine to the nearest hospital. She hoped Randy would be back before the end of the two-hour tour. Otherwise, Willow and Jane promised to get their group back to the hotel. She felt terrible for having to ask them; this was supposed to be a romantic getaway, not an extra job.

After a long wait in a busy waiting room, a doctor, who luckily spoke English, ushered them into his office.

"I feel so foolish. I work with animals all the time; I don't know what went wrong," Sabine said sheepishly. "It must be the jet lag."

The doctor nodded. "Unfortunately, dog bites are not uncommon. Last year half a million Parisians were bitten by a dog, and about sixty thousand of them were hospitalized. And when it is a feral or abandoned dog, we always advise rabies shots. It is good that you have already had your first set. You only need two more: one today and the second in three days' time. If you return to this clinic, we can administer it for you. Or will you be back in the United States?"

"No, we are here for six more days. I'll have to come back."

Lana rose. "Excuse me; I need to use the toilet. Can I meet you back in the lobby when you are done, Sabine?"

Sabine nodded. "Sure. Thanks again for coming with me, Lana."

"No problem, it's all part of the job." Though Lana was smiling, she was internally fuming that she was missing their tour of the Louvre. With a little luck, she could reserve a ticket on one of their free afternoons.

"Doctor, which way is the toilet?"

"Let me show you. I have to get the rabies booster. It's in the medical storage room next door."

They exited the doctor's office and turned to the left. At the end of the hall were the toilets and the supply room. Lana thanked the doctor and went inside. She took her time, wanting a moment to freshen up.

When she left the bathroom minutes later, Sabine was in the hallway. But she wasn't coming out of the doctor's office. It seemed like she was exiting the medical supply room.

That's odd, Lana thought, just as the other woman appeared to notice her.

"Oh, there's the bathroom," said Sabine with a laugh. "I've had the shot. I'll be right out, okay?"

"Take your time," Lana said. *Sabine must be a bit confused thanks to the stress of the dog bite and shot*, she thought. Although when Lana turned to look back at the closing bathroom door, she realized the toilet sign was quite large and hard to miss. Sabine would have walked right past it to get to the supply room.

Lana was staring at the doors, puzzled, when Sabine exited the bathroom. "Should we meet up with the others now?"

"Sure," Lana said. They walked outside and took a taxi back to the Louvre. Sabine told her all about her animal shelters and clinic, while showing her photos of her favorite strays. As she paid their taxi driver, Lana looked at her watch and realized the tour was ending in five minutes. There wasn't even enough time to actually go inside. Instead, they stood close to the exit, waiting for her group to emerge from the glass pyramid.

Apparently Randy had made it back in time because he was the first one she spotted coming out of the museum. He walked over to her, a grin on his face. "It's too bad you missed the tour, Lana. I don't know much about art, but I do know that what they have on display is top class," he said enthusiastically.

Lana thought of all the masterworks hanging on those walls, many considered to be the *crème de la crème* of art history, and sighed. *Next time.*

13

Fountains and Food Markets

Lana stopped to let a mother pushing a baby carriage pass, smiling at the beautiful infant as they did. Her group was attempting to cross Rue de Bretagne, a busy shopping street, on their way to the next stop on this morning's tour. Their guide had just shown them the Stravinsky Fountain, an incredible collection of mechanized statues placed in a long, oval pool of water. The makers, French artists Niki de Saint Phalle and Jean Tinguely, had created the colorful moving lips, musical notes, dancing mermaid, heart, and more as an homage to composer Igor Stravinsky. Lana had never seen anything like it and was charmed by how the brightly painted creations danced in the water. Not all of her guests were as enchanted with the sculptures, she realized when she overheard Henry joking with Edward about wasting public money on this kind of crap.

The mechanical fountain was perfectly placed across from the futuristic Centre Pompidou. It was one of the oddest buildings Lana had ever seen. The escalators and staircases of the multistory building were on the outside of the structure, and surrounded by plastic tubes that reminded Lana of a giant hamster cage.

After a brief explanation about the fountain's history and that of the star-crossed lovers who created it, their guide led them to the day's culinary highlight—the Marché des Enfants Rouges. It took more time than their guide expected to walk from the fountain to the food market, simply because

Sabine stopped to pet pretty much every leashed animal they came across. She even took a few selfies with some of the better-dressed pooches. If her husband hadn't gently pulled her along, they may have never made it.

Lana was looking forward to their next stop. Having grown up with the expansive, open-air Pike Place Market, Lana had high expectations of this French equivalent. Unfortunately, they were quickly dashed as soon as she stepped through the green entrance gates. It was tiny. Apparently Lana was not the only one. A wave of disappointed sighs emitted from their group as they regathered inside the market. Only Angie and Bernie, two recent transplants to Seattle, seemed delighted.

Their guide must have sensed the majority's disappointment. "Welcome to Marché des Enfants Rouges, the oldest food market in Paris, and what most consider the gastronomic highlight of the city. It may be small, but it is packed full of the best meats, cheeses, and produce you will find in France," he explained, his voice cheery as he made eye contact with all of his guests.

"It was established in 1628 and takes its name from the old orphanage this building once housed. 'Enfants Rouges' refers to the children's red clothes, the color of which indicated the garments were donated by Christian charities. Here you will find fresh products, butchers, fishmongers, cheese makers, florists, and a selection of restaurants and food stands from all over the world. Traditional French dishes are served alongside Japanese, Moroccan, and Caribbean specialties."

"Oooh, that sounds like my kind of food," Bernie said, patting his ample stomach.

"Great, I expected traditional French cuisine to be served here, not fusion or international dishes. We are in France, aren't we?" Chad said, rather severely.

The guide looked at him, puzzled. "Of course, sir. Most of the produce served here is locally grown, and the restaurants offer a wide selection of traditional dishes. But Paris is a multicultural city, just as most major cities are. Sometimes the combinations of old and new produce fascinating results."

"That's exactly what I think," Bernie said, nodding. "We're going to get along just fine."

"Humph, we'll see," Chad said and slunk away to a produce stand.

The guide didn't know what to do. He looked to Randy, who looked to Lana, who motioned for the guide to continue. "We have a special tour planned of the market before we sample dishes served by the many restaurants you will find inside," he said.

Lana listened to the guide, yet she was watching Chad as he pointed to baskets of raspberries and blueberries, then held up euros in place of speaking. The merchant packed up his fruit and bade him *merci* before Chad rejoined the group.

As their guide ushered them into the crowded, narrow aisles, Lana pushed images of Pike Place Market out of her mind and looked around again with new eyes. It may have been smaller than she expected after all the hype, but the atmosphere was entertaining and lively.

Miranda caught up with Chad, who was stuffing himself with fresh fruit. She took one of the blueberries and immediately cringed. "Jeez, those are sour! I don't know how you can eat them."

"That is how they are supposed to taste. That store-bought fruit has ruined your taste buds," he said dismissively, polishing off the last handful in one gulp. He then pushed his way to the front of the group, determined to be the first to taste the many samples the vendors were providing. Miranda watched him walk away, a confused expression on her face.

They followed their guide through the maze of stalls. Long skylights running the length of the roof provided plenty of light. Fresh produce and herbs were displayed in pretty, woven reed baskets and crates. Lana marveled at the size of the produce. She had never seen such large pumpkins, onions, or tomatoes before. Most stands proudly claimed to be *biologiques* or biological. She could imagine most of her group would appreciate that.

Their guide took them into the next aisle. Enormous wheels of cheese were lined up behind glass display cases, directly across from a flower shop. A long line of people waiting to order at a takeaway restaurant farther up the aisle made navigating the narrow aisles rather challenging. But the wonderful smells mixing together made the jostling and slow tempo a pleasure, not a problem. Lana took in the selections of one of the more popular cafés as she passed. The pottery plates heaped full of fresh salads, sausages, and pasta looked so delicious.

They stopped at several merchants, sampling fresh herbs, cheeses, sausages, olives, and breads spread out on large platters. Lana was not a foodie, but what she was consuming was so much better than the products she bought at supermarkets back home. She had to restrain herself from taking the last bites of the dishes, allowing her guests to finish the scrumptious food instead.

Miranda, Tamara, and her husband, Edward, seemed the least interested in the tour, only trying a few bites here and there. Edward spent more time looking at his phone than the market stalls, while Miranda and Tamara preferred the flowers and plants to the food.

Randy was at the back of the group, chatting easily with Henry and Chad. She was glad he was here to entertain the men. Though Chad had done what he promised and treated her as a complete stranger, Lana was still a little uncomfortable being around him. The only saving grace was that he had apparently lied about more than just his job description and marital status. He was not the caring, sweet man she had met in Seattle, but a distant and cold person with more interest in his notebook than his wife. Why, she still did not know, but he continued pulling it out to jot down notes about the food and drinks he consumed. It was an unusual habit.

When they reached a slightly quieter section, Lana called out to her group, "Before I forget—I want to pick up a selection of cheeses and sausages to take with us on our picnic. If anyone has any suggestions, please do let me know. Wanderlust Tours is buying."

Bernie piped up immediately. "Could you pick up a blue cheese, maybe a Fourme d'Ambert or Bleu du Vercors? Those are my favorites and will go well with the baguettes we're going to make."

"No, that's a rookie mistake," Chad said, as he worked his way to the front of the group. "It's better to pair a baguette with a Camembert or Brie. The creamy texture contrasts nicely with the crispiness of the baguette. Blues should be paired with rye bread."

Bernie puffed up his chest as he approached Chad. "My choice is more adventurous, that's all."

"It's a question of taste, and whether you have any or not. You obviously do not have a refined palate if you enjoy eating a blue with a baguette," Chad snapped.

"You sound just like that pompous critic my friends in Florida warned me about, The Fussy Gourmet. He's got a column in the *Seattle Chronicle*—the Chef's Delight, or something like that."

"Chef's Special," Chad corrected.

"So you do read that drivel."

Chad's eyes widened so quickly, Lana was afraid they were going to pop out of his head. Why would he care what Bernie thought about a Seattle food critic?

"Chad, honey, can you take a look at this, please?" Miranda took his arm, leading him away from Bernie.

Even after Chad was out of eyesight, Bernie's face remained flushed red, and his eyes were bulging. He was livid, Lana realized. *Why would he get so worked up about a cheese?*

Angie grabbed his arms and started doing a breathing exercise with him. Lana shook her head in confusion. This group was so competitive with each other, it was difficult to be around them. At least Willow and Jane appeared to be getting along better.

After her group had woven its way through the maze of stalls, their guide led them back outside to an alleyway filled with long tables. Plastic tents with see-through curtains protected diners against the cold. Three tables were already filled with several sample platters from the restaurants inside the market.

Chad took a seat close to the middle so that he could easily reach all of the dishes and pulled out his trusty notepad.

"I hope you enjoyed your tour of the market?" their guide asked, receiving a round of enthusiastic nods in affirmation. "Excellent. Here we have several dishes for you to sample. All are sold by cafés in the market. In addition to traditional French cuisine, we also have samples of the international dishes available, many of which are fused with local recipes."

"Count me out. I'll stick with the pure cuisine," Chad said.

"What do you have against fusion?" Bernie demanded.

Lana couldn't believe it. She had never met anyone so worked up about a food tasting. What was wrong with these two?

"Angie and I are about to open up our first fusion restaurant, and the reactions so far have been spectacularly positive."

Chad laughed. "By who—your Florida friends? Has anyone of substance sampled your dishes? What are you going to serve anyway?"

Angie jutted out her chin. "Dishes from around the world served in small portions, so diners can easily share them. That's why we're on this tour, to find more inspirations for dishes we could serve."

"That sounds wonderful. What are you calling it?" Willow asked.

"Global Nibbles." Angie beamed. "I thought that up. But wait until you hear the best part! We've designed it so the kitchen is in the middle, with tables placed around it. Instead of ordering individual dishes, the cooks make up several and place them on a conveyor belt. Customers pick the food off of it, as it rolls by. It looks so futuristic! We were inspired by a dim sum restaurant we went to in Tokyo. It was really fun watching the food travel around the room. We ended up sampling everything," she oozed in enthusiasm.

Chad began laughing. "What a horrible name. I suppose it's fitting for your terrible concept."

"Why you –" Bernie lunged at Chad, his arms stretching towards his throat, when Randy grabbed him and held him back.

"Hey guys, there is no reason to get so worked up about this. Everyone has different tastes," Randy said.

"We've invested our life savings in this venture. How can you be so cruel?" Angie asked, tears forming in her eyes as she admonished Chad.

"That's a shame. You should have stayed in Florida."

"Who do you think you are, talking to me like that?" Bernie said.

"Fusion does not deserve a place in any restaurant. It's the purity of the recipe and the chef's ability to work within the local culinary restraints that make traditional recipes timeless. Fusion food may be hip and trendy, but you won't see anyone serving that drivel in a hundred years. *Foie gras, coq au vin*, beef bourguignon, and soufflés will always be on menus."

"Says you. Who died and made you a food god, anyway?"

"According to the *USA Today*, I'm one of the best restaurant critics in the nation. For the last ten years running."

"Who are you?" Bernie asked.

"Your worst nightmare. I'm the pompous jerk your friends warned you about."

Bernie's face drained of color. "You're The Fussy Gourmet? Could it get any worse?"

Chad winked at him. "Wait until opening day. I'll be there with bells on. And my review will have you closing down within a week."

"How can you say that? We haven't even opened yet!" Bernie raged.

"It doesn't matter—I can tell it's going to be rubbish. And you must know it subconsciously, too, because you have already included a trash belt in your design."

"How dare you! What do you know about running a restaurant?" Bernie countered. His neck was getting so red, Lana grew concerned about his health. Angie must have, too, because she grabbed his arm and tried pulling him away from Chad. It didn't work. "Critiquing food is one thing, but training staff and maintaining quality takes a lot more effort than sampling a few bites and scribbling about it."

"I happen to know quite a bit about how to run a restaurant; in fact I'm in the process of opening one now," Chad responded, his voice full of pride.

Miranda grabbed his arm. "What? Why didn't you tell me?"

"We'll speak about it later," Chad said, as he broke free from her grip, his attention focused on degrading Bernie.

"No, we'll speak about it now. I thought we agreed you were going to wait."

Chad seemed to forget all about Bernie. He turned to his wife. "I don't want to do this in front of your friends."

"How could you open a restaurant without telling me?" she pleaded.

Chad leaned his forehead against hers, but his voice was still audible to the group. "Miranda, there are a lot of things I haven't told you lately. Ever since Daniel died, it's like I can hear a clock ticking. I can't help but wonder how much time I have left. And all I know is that I don't want to spend the rest of my life worrying about what your family thinks. We're both turning sixty this year. How much longer do we have to wait to do what we want, instead of what your father dictates?"

Miranda shook her head. "I know how hard it is for you, Daniel dying so unexpectedly. But we've always been there for each other. We can get through this."

"I don't know," Chad mumbled and stepped back. "I'm so confused. I need some time to think. I'll see you later, back at the hotel." He took her hand and squeezed it, before walking away in a daze.

Miranda watched him go, tears forming in her eyes. Moments later she raced into the market. Sabine broke free from her husband's grip and chased after her friend.

"Come on, Chad. That's no way to treat your wife. Tomorrow is Valentine's Day," Henry, Sabine's husband, called out.

Chad turned to him, an odd grin on his face. "What do you know about life or love, Henry? At least I know that my marriage is a sham."

Henry looked at him as if he was crazy. "What are you talking about?"

Tamara stepped in between them. "Chad, that's enough. You have no right to judge Sabine or Miranda. They've been friends forever."

"Sure, 'friends,'" Chad said, then stalked out of the market and back onto the busy Rue de Bretagne.

"Why can't he accept that we love each other like sisters?" Sabine asked her husband, shaking her head.

What a nightmare, Lana thought. "Randy, can you stay with the group while I talk to Miranda and Sabine?"

"No problem, Lana. Folks, there is a gorgeous selection of dishes for us to sample. Who wants to dig in first?" he said, rubbing his palms together.

Lana knew they would be in good hands. She hated to interrupt Miranda and Sabine, but after lunch, they had a guided tour at the Picasso Museum a few streets further up. She could imagine Miranda would want to take some time for herself, and Lana wouldn't be surprised if Sabine wanted to stay with her. The two ladies were quite close.

She soon found them at the back of the market. Sabine held her friend tight as Miranda softly wept on her shoulder. "He has no right," Lana heard Miranda say, as she approached. "I've given up everything for him, even children, and he treats me like a sack of dirt."

"Why don't you leave him? You two are worse when you're together, not better. You were the one who helped me realize that no one has to stay in a bad relationship."

"You know I can't."

"Money isn't everything, Miranda," Sabine reprimanded her.

Miranda's weeping intensified.

Sabine was rocking her gently and murmuring to her when she noticed Lana approaching. "Lana, did Chad come back?"

"No, I'm sorry, he didn't. I'm not sure where he went."

Miranda's crying intensified. "How could he do this to me?"

Lana looked to the ground, wishing she could be anywhere but here. "I'm so sorry. I'll leave you two alone, but I first need to find out what you want to do. The group needs to leave in a few minutes and head over to the Picasso Museum for our next tour. If you would rather not join us, I can ask Randy to escort you back to the hotel." Lana didn't know what else she could do for Miranda other than give her space.

Miranda nodded.

"I think that's a great idea. Chad will be back soon. He always comes back," Sabine added, looking at Lana as she spoke. Lana couldn't tell whether Sabine was happy or saddened by this fact.

"Great, I'll tell Randy where you're at." As much as Lana wanted to comfort Miranda, all she felt was shame for kissing Chad back in Seattle.

Lana returned to her group, glad to see the rest appeared to be getting along and acting as if nothing had happened. Even Bernie was back to his jovial, carefree self, sitting with his arm tossed over Angie's shoulder, a large plate of food before him.

"I tell you what, this trip has been a godsend. We've gotten so many great ideas for new dishes," Bernie said, his mouth full of couscous.

"That's wonderful, Bernie," Lana said, adding, "Randy, can I talk to you?"

"Sure, Lana," he walked with her, away from their group's table. "Miranda and Sabine want to go back to the hotel and wait for Chad. Would you mind escorting them back? You can hail a taxi."

"Great, I'll take care of it," Randy said and walked with purpose into the market. Soon Lana saw the three of them walking out the gate and back into the busy streets of the Marais district.

Lana scooped up a bite of each dish, savoring the mix of herbs and spices. It was quite a treat for her taste buds. As she lifted the last bite to her mouth, her phone began to vibrate. She set down her plate and addressed the group. "Who's ready to see the Picasso Museum? They have a new exhibition that is getting rave reviews. It features paintings Pablo Picasso made of his many muses."

"You mean lovers, right?" Angie asked, making doe eyes at her husband before rubbing her nose against his.

"Too bad Chad left. Sounds right up his alley," Edward sniggered.

Tamara slapped his chest. "Hey, that was private," she admonished.

"What? Miranda's not here."

Tamara shook her head and looked away.

Lana wondered again whether she was the only "distraction" Chad had flirted with on Seattle Singles. From the sound of it, she was not his first girlfriend on the side. As their guide led her group back out onto the main street, all Lana could think was, *How could I be so foolish?*

14

Last-Minute Changes

Lana splashed cold water on her face, wanting to be fully awake while reading through the tour notes for her group's next stops, when there was a knock on her door.

After their chaotic market tour, she half-expected to see Bernie on the other side, ready to apologize for blowing a fuse. Not that he should feel obligated, given that Chad had instigated the argument. She hoped he and Miranda had found time to talk; it sounded like they had a lot to work through. And there was already enough marital squabbling going on. When she had been assigned to this lovers-only tour, she'd expected to be dodging public displays of affection between her guests, not to have to play referee to their arguments.

When she opened the door, the person she least expected to see was standing there, looking quite uncomfortable. "Hi Sabine, how are you doing?"

Sabine glanced at her bandaged hand. "The bite is healing well, I think. I don't hurt as much when I move it."

"That's a good sign," Lana said. "And Miranda? How is she holding up? Did Chad return?"

"He did, and they talked, though she's not ready to confide in me. Whatever he said upset her, but she'll be okay once she's had some time to cool off. She and Chad may not have had the best marriage, but they have been together for thirty-six years. They'll get through it. Henry is watching sports down in the bar with Randy so we can have some girl time."

"That's nice of him. If there is anything I can do for her, please let me know." Lana smiled and began to close the door, hoping to get started on her homework for the night. The guests had a night off to do something romantic, though Lana was beginning to doubt that many of her couples would actually do so.

Sabine stayed put.

"Can I help you with anything?"

"I haven't thanked you for your help at the hospital. And for asking Randy to take us back to the hotel."

"It's no problem; all in a day's work."

Sabine remained in the doorway.

"Would you like to come in?" Lana asked, hoping to prod her guest into action.

"No, I should get back to Miranda. But I did want to ask if it was too late to make a change to the itinerary."

Lana groaned internally. Dotty did place a large emphasis on how tour participants could have a say in the group's scheduled activities. But Lana was fairly certain she meant before the tour began.

"What did you have in mind?" she asked, keeping her tone even, hoping Sabine's request wasn't too difficult to realize.

"Some friends back home were here last month and took a baking workshop with another baker, Pierre le Monde. They say he's the best and wondered why we hadn't booked his class."

Oh, no, Lana thought. "Honestly, I don't know why this baker was chosen. The arrangements were booked ahead of time by someone working in the office. I do know it was difficult to schedule any workshop because most were full."

"My friends just keep raving about him, his techniques, and how good he is with his students. Pierre sounds like a wonderful teacher. We sure would love to take a class with him," Sabine insisted.

Lana frowned. Why was she pushing so hard for this change? It was a three-hour class, not a week of intensive training; did it really matter who gave the lessons? But the Wanderlust Tours staff motto went through Lana's head: *Happy clients leave five-star reviews.* She recharged her smile. "Let me see what I can do."

"Thanks," Sabine said. She looked so relieved.

"No promises," Lana quickly added.

"Sure, I understand. But thanks for trying. Miranda will be thrilled."

"Is there anything else I can do for you?"

"No, the workshop is enough."

Sabine started to walk away when Lana called out, "Are they going to be okay? Or do I need to arrange an extra room for Chad?"

"That won't be necessary. They've broken up more times than I can count, but she always lets him come back." Sabine sounded bitter. "She has to," she added softly.

That's an odd thing to say, Lana thought. Before she could try to get more information out of her, Miranda opened the door to Sabine's room and poked her head out. *Her ears must be burning*, Lana thought.

"Did you ask her?" Miranda said, clearly focused on her friend. Miranda's eyes were swollen and her cheeks puffy.

In a gentle voice, Sabine said, "It's taken care of. I'll be right back." She nodded at Lana. "Let me know about the workshop, okay?"

"Sure," Lana said as her guest walked back to her friend.

15

Travel Time

"Hi, Lana. How's it going?" Dotty asked. Through the video feed, Lana could see that her boss was sitting on her couch with two dogs and a cat on her lap. Thanks to the animals' varied shades of fur and the intertwining of their bodies, it looked like Dotty was covered in a patchwork quilt of affection.

"Pretty well," Lana fibbed, wanting to keep their conversation upbeat.

"How is Randy working out?"

"He is navigationally challenged, but quite good with the guests. He's a keeper."

"If you say so, that's good enough for me. Thanks for taking him under your wing."

"It's no problem. He's a nice guy," Lana responded automatically before realizing she had actually meant what she said. Sure, he was a bit eager to please, but that enthusiasm would be tempered by experience, she reckoned. And he did have a way of putting even the most sour clients and waitstaff at ease, which was a vital skill of a tour guide.

"Are the guests getting along?"

"You were right about the group dynamic," Lana replied, dodging Dotty's question. "The three couples tend to stick together. Angie and Bernie probably would feel left out if Willow and Jane weren't here. So far, they have been hanging out quite a bit during the tours and seem to be getting along."

Now, Lana added in her mind. After a rough start, even Jane seemed to be succumbing to Angie and Bernie's charms. As intense as they were, the two Floridians were interesting people and fun to be around.

"I sure hope so. Bernie's new conveyor belt restaurant is opening up in Fremont next month, a few doors down from her yoga studio."

"What? He didn't mention that he was moving to Fremont."

"Oh, I'm surprised. Though to be honest, I only know because he is renting one of my spaces to open up his latest venture."

"Wait, this isn't his first restaurant?"

"From what my property manager tells me, he had a string of successful restaurants in Florida. But then he had a breakdown and sold them all. I'm not sure how he ended up in Seattle."

"Huh, they come across as so carefree and, frankly, irresponsible. I didn't see them being with it enough to run a successful business."

"Whoa, that's rather harsh!" Dotty laughed.

"They are really nice people," Lana blushed. "I'm just surprised, that's all."

"Fair enough. I'm glad to hear things are working out."

"I do have one question," Lana asked hesitantly.

"Okay—shoot!"

"Sabine just stopped by to ask if we could book them into a different baguette workshop."

"She what?" Dotty's voice rose in disbelief. Rodney groggily raised his head at the interruption. Dotty stroked her pug's back, which made his tail flicker, which woke up Lana's cat. Seymour rose and stretched his back out, causing Chipper to roll off of Dotty's lap and wake with a start. "Woof," he complained, before jumping back up onto the couch and lying down next to his mistress.

"Sorry, dears. They have been sleeping like this at night on my bed, too. They kept fighting over my second pillow, so I had to buy two more so that we can all get a good night's sleep. Isn't that right, boys?" she said, snuggling with all three before addressing Lana again.

"You know, you try to be accommodating, but enough is enough. This is the last time I encourage the guests to make suggestions. They are eating up my profit margin."

Lana had wondered why Dotty was being so accommodating. She figured it was because of the media coverage her tours had received. The tours were quite expensive, but the clients were treated as royalty for the duration. The luxurious hotels, dinners, and private tours did cost quite a bit. And the extras added up quickly. Lana had been shocked to see the tickets for the Moulin Rouge alone were almost three hundred dollars per person.

"What irks me most is that Sabine is the one who requested—no, demanded—that their group take a workshop with that other baker. I had to pay double because he was already booked out for the month. Why does she want to change bakers now?"

"Apparently friends back home are raving about this Pierre le Monde guy. They took a baguette workshop with him last month," Lana explained while Dotty shook her head in irritation. "I could lie and say he is full."

Dotty rose slowly, allowing the animals a chance to reposition themselves on the couch. "And what happens if she calls and finds out that he is not? No, you had better get in touch and see if he can fit your group in. I would do it, but the time difference makes it challenging."

Dotty walked through her living room towards her office and rummaged around her desk. "Here's your itinerary. The workshop is set for the day after tomorrow. If this other baker is as good as they say, I can imagine he is fully booked." Dotty drummed her fingers on her lower lip, considering. "I'm willing to pay double his going rate, but not a penny more. If he doesn't agree, then tell your group that he was full. That's all we can do."

"Okay, I'll do my best to make it happen."

"I know you will, Lana, and I'm grateful," Dotty said, her tone sincere. She checked the itinerary again, squinting to read it properly. "It looks like your group has the evening free."

"Luckily, they do," Lana said, then quickly added, "It will give me a chance to call Sabine's baker." *And decompress from this morning's horrible market tour,* she thought, not wanting to say the words aloud. Dotty didn't need to know all the details right now. After she got back to Seattle, she could regal Dotty with some of the funnier stories. The nasty arguments and conflicts didn't need to be rehashed. At least their tour of the Picasso Museum had gone smoothly; after Chad's departure, everyone had seemed to get along quite well.

"And tomorrow is that horticulture tour. I'll be curious to see what you think of the Jardin des Plantes. I bet it will make a great post for your Travel Time blog."

"You're right, I'll have to take my camera along." Working for Dotty as a tour guide had boosted her self-confidence so much that Lana had recently taken up writing again, and her new job provided the perfect source material. Her guests' comments about how they wished bloggers would show more of the reality of travel, instead of just touched-up selfies, had inspired Lana to do just that. Her blog was only a few weeks old, but it was already generating hundreds of hits a day. Visitors responded positively to her detailed summaries about the individual sites they visited on their tours, as well as her plethora of photos showing exactly what tourists could expect to see and experience on their journey—and all without a single selfie. The last thing she wanted was for one of her old colleagues to stumble upon her site. Being wrongly accused of libel and then fired for it was an open wound that would never heal.

Seymour sauntered into the office and meowed. Dotty picked him up and sat in her office chair. His purrs made Lana feel right at home.

"Don't forget to treat yourself to a nice dinner tonight," Dotty said, stroking her cat's velvety black fur. "Maybe you and Randy can go somewhere fancy. You've got my list of recommended restaurants, right?"

"I do. That's a really good idea, Dotty. I'll catch up with Randy after I call that baker. I don't know if I would dare eat alone at any of the places on your list. A table for one isn't so romantic, and it is the day before Valentine's Day."

"Don't you worry about what other people think. You have as much right to a great meal as any couple does. If Randy won't join you, take a good book along and ask for a table by the window—that's what I always did on my free evenings. Sometimes it's better to take time for yourself."

Lana was shocked. Dotty was one of the most social people she knew. Up until now, she couldn't imagine her boss wanting to eat alone anywhere.

Lana and Ron had done everything together during their marriage. And since their split, she'd stopped going out to dinner or clubs unless a friend invited her to tag along. Maybe a table for one was in order tonight.

"Good luck tomorrow," Dotty said.

Lana tapped the screen. "Thanks, Dotty. Give my boy a kiss for me. Talk to you soon."

16

Lana Gets Curious

Lana turned on her laptop so she could look up the baker Sabine was so keen on. While she waited for the older machine to warm up, snippets of the day's many conflicts flashed through her mind. From her extensive experience as a kayaking guide, she knew that the stress inherent to traveling tended to bring out tensions within a group. This tour, however, was proving to be the extreme.

Was the lovers theme putting too much pressure on the couples? Was that why Chad was acting like such a jerk? So far, he was far more interested in writing in his little notebook than spending time with his wife. Miranda was apparently used to it because she gravitated towards Sabine, making her husband the third wheel. And as much as Tamara and Edward were passionate about each other, they spent very little time actually talking to one another. Edward preferred his smartphone and stock prices to romancing his wife. The tour was not at all what Lana was expecting.

So far, only Angie and Bernie appeared to be truly happy together. Willow and Jane seemed to have relaxed more, but Lana was afraid it was only a temporary truce. Lana hoped her friends soon figured out what was most important to them, before this baby war tore them apart.

Bernie had lost his cool during the market tour, which Lana thought seemed quite out of character for him. Why were Bernie and Angie so concerned about what Chad thought? Sure, he claimed to be an important restaurant critic. That would explain how he'd known about the best restaurants in Seattle, Lana realized, thinking back on their picnic in Gas Works Park. But Angie and Bernie were so laid back about everything. And Lana couldn't imagine that one bad review could really close a restaurant, no matter what Bernie thought.

Who were Angie and Bernie, really? Lana doubted they were the hippie couple they claimed to be. The photos in Angie's album spoke of a different past. Lana wondered how much business sense they had. Why would they invest all of their money into a crazy new restaurant venture? Conveyor belts did sound futuristic and fun, but would such an idea even make it past the strict health code regulations? Trendy restaurants tended to do well in Seattle only until the next trend arrived. And Angie's clunky attempts to sell crystals to other members of the tour were just embarrassing.

Miranda's reaction to Chad's announcement about opening a restaurant was quite unexpected. It was clearly a bombshell for her, though Lana couldn't think of why. Whoever Daniel was, his death had deeply affected Chad. Was his confrontation with mortality the reason why he'd signed up for the Seattle Singles dating site? Lana frowned. She would almost think so, if it weren't for Edward's snide comment about him being a playboy. Yet, if it was true, why would Miranda stay with him? She seemed smart enough to know she could find another partner in life. Lana doubted it had anything to do with money; surely a restaurant critic couldn't earn that much.

Lana felt a to-do list coming on. She pulled out a notebook and wrote down all of her questions about her clients. She had never met such a volatile group of people before and wanted to get a better idea of who exactly she was spending the week with. Once she'd filled the page, she turned to her laptop and set to work. Instead of looking up the contact information for the baker, Pierre le Monde, she started with the first question on her list.

As she expected, she could not find any reference to The Fussy Gourmet's identity, meaning she had to take Chad's word for it. His future restaurant was as much a mystery. It made sense, she thought, imagining that he would prefer to keep it secret until it was about to open.

Lana's jaw dropped when she googled Bernie's name. Dotty was well-informed. Her pudgy, happy-go-lucky client was in fact the owner of several Michelin-starred restaurants in Miami and Tampa Bay, Florida. Well, he had been, until he sold them six months ago and disappeared. At least, that's how several society columns described his exit from the local scene. There were rumors that he had opened up a chain of restaurants in Europe; others suspected he had suffered a burnout and retired to the Florida Keys. Apparently the newspapers in Florida didn't know he was now in Seattle.

As Lana looked at photos of Bernie in a suit, she had trouble reconciling the images of this suave and sophisticated businessman with her guest. Whatever had happened, Bernie had gone through a major transformation in a short amount of time. She made a note to ask Angie and Bernie about their life in Florida, when and if she had the chance to do so casually. As much as she longed to satisfy her curiosity, she didn't want to make her guests uncomfortable. For some reason, they had turned their backs on their past and were starting over. It wasn't Lana's place to put them on the spot about it.

As last, Lana typed Miranda's name into the search engine. Several articles about her horticulture club and its work in Volunteer Park appeared, but not much else. On the third page of the search results, Lana found a link to her marriage announcement—thirty-six years earlier. She and Chad had been college sweethearts. They had gotten married in Pullman, Washington, home to the university where they'd met as students. In the photo they both looked so young and happy. It broke Lana's heart to think of what they had become. Miranda's maid of honor looked familiar, but Lana couldn't place her, until she read the caption. It was Sabine! *Wow, they have known each other for years*, Lana thought.

She re-read the caption, her brain sticking on Miranda's maiden name. It seemed so familiar. She started to type it in, when a knock on her door broke her concentration. When she looked through the peephole, she was not surprised to see it was Randy.

"Hi, what can I do for you?"

Randy looked as eager and nervous as ever. He stood before her, his baseball cap in hand. "Our guests are all out enjoying their free evening.

Would you like to have dinner with me?"

Lana smiled, and she could tell it immediately set him at ease. As much as she appreciated Dotty's advice, she was glad Randy dared to ask her to join him again. Not only would she feel more relaxed having a table companion, but it would also be a good way to get to know him better. If Dotty did hire him, then they were probably going to be spending a lot of time with each other. The Wanderlust team of tour guides was a close-knit group of unique individuals who often hung out together when they were in Seattle.

"That sounds wonderful, Randy. Let me get my coat."

17

Jardin des Plantes

February 14—Day Three of the Wanderlust Tour in Paris, France

Things were going so well today. Lana's group had spent their morning on a bus and walking tour of the city center, visiting the sites featured on most postcards. What surprised her most was how the more famous monuments were squished in between residential neighborhoods and busy streets. Most shocking to Lana was discovering that the Arc de Triomphe stood in the middle of a busy traffic circle. Surrounded by beeping horns and exhaust fumes was not how she imagined seeing this incredible memorial dedicated to those who had lost their lives fighting for France.

As they explored Pont Neuf, Sainte-Chapelle, Notre Dame, the Shakespeare & Company bookstore, and the Panthéon, Lana thought about how surreal it was to be in this city, one featured so often in movies and television shows— so much so that it felt as if she'd walked these streets before.

The view from the Notre Dame towers was the high point of the morning for Lana, and definitely worth walking up the 422 steps to experience. From their high vantage point, they could see most of Paris, the long boulevards dissecting the city, the taller monuments, and the large green parks. The many gargoyles placed on the towers found their way into her pictures. Their dark bodies and horrifying expressions contrasted well with the buildings far below, bathed in the yellowish-hues of the morning sun.

Her guests were in a surprisingly good mood, considering how explosive the market tour had been yesterday. An evening free was apparently what everyone needed.

Miranda and Sabine walked arm in arm, while Henry and Randy trailed closely behind. From what Lana could hear, both men were sports fans and bonded over the Seattle Mariners. Walking behind them were Tamara and Edward. She pointed out every haute couture shop to her friends, and he kept one eye on the smartphone in his right hand. *How can he walk without tripping?* Lana wondered.

Willow and Jane seemed to be happy, as well. They chatted easily with Bernie and Angie; both couples seemed to enjoy the same things and had similar positions on many current issues. Lana was tempted to tell Willow that Bernie's restaurant would be opening close to her studio in a few months, but she figured it was better if he told her instead. She only had Dotty's hearsay information; perhaps he hadn't actually signed the rental contract yet.

Trailing far behind the rest was Chad. He had shown up in the lobby at the last minute and silently entered the bus, sitting far away from Miranda. Whatever they had discussed last night had not made his wife happy. Edward did his best to avoid Chad, their scuffle at the pond obviously not forgotten. Bernie ignored Chad resolutely, rewarded by his wife with little pats and cuddles of encouragement.

After their tour of the Panthéon, their guide pointed Lana towards their next stop, the Jardin des Plantes, before bidding them *adieu.*

Lana readjusted her backpack. It was heavier than normal because she had brought along her good camera. This morning alone she had taken hundreds of photos. Selecting just a handful to share on her blog was going to be difficult.

As they approached the Place Monge metro station, Lana said, "Now, gang, in a few minutes our guided tour of Jardin des Plantes will begin. It is a special treat for the horticulturists among us, but not required."

"I'm so excited to see this place," Angie gushed, clapping her hands together. "I started studying herbal medicine recently and can't wait to hear what the guide can teach us."

"That's wonderful, Angie," Lana said with a smile. She was grateful for the older woman's enthusiasm. "However, if anyone does not want to join the tour, please let me know. Technically, this is your free afternoon. The gardens are a few streets away. Anyone who is not interested in joining the tour can take the metro or a taxi back to the hotel. We just ask that you be in the lobby a few minutes before five. A taxi will take us over to the champagne tasting, then at 7 p.m. we will head over to the Moulin Rouge for dinner and the show."

Willow raised her hand.

"I booked you and Jane into Chez Paris at seven," Lana confirmed. Willow and Jane nodded at each other in satisfaction.

"Angie, Bernie, have you made a decision about tonight?"

"Yes, we are going to a rub-in."

"A what?"

"A spiritual center is organizing it. There's going to be live music and a vegetarian buffet. After dinner, we all sit in a circle and give each other back massages. It's a wonderful way to get grounded and feel connected to our fellow humans," Angie explained.

"Ah, okay. That sounds interesting."

"I'm not into plants; that's her thing," Edward said. "I'll see you back at the hotel. Okay, babe?" He pulled Tamara in tight and kissed her on the lips. Before she could respond, he took out his phone and began texting while walking away.

"Anyone else want to skip it?" Lana asked.

"Why do you think this is open for discussion? I told you, I am not closing my business. If you won't agree to work less, then there is no reason to make the IVF appointment. Period." Willow's rising voice wafted over the group.

Lana rolled her eyes. *Just when things appeared to be getting better*, she thought.

"If you can't work this out, maybe you two shouldn't have kids. It only gets harder," Chad said.

"Excuse me? What gives you the right to comment on our relationship?"

Jane asked, hands on her hips.

Miranda snorted. "Yeah, Chad. What do you know about kids? You refused to father any."

"Exactly for this reason."

"Stay out of our business," Jane stated, standing on her toes to address him.

"It's rather difficult to ignore your problems when you keep broadcasting them to the group."

"Ha! You're one to talk," Jane retorted.

Chad's eyes narrowed. "I'm not interested in joining the plant tour either, Lana." It was the first time he had addressed her during the trip. Hearing him say her name made her feel dirty. "I'll see you later, Miranda," Chad said, then walked away without showing her a single sign of affection.

That poor woman, Lana thought, *what a horrible Valentine's Day*. Lana was again amazed at how different this Chad was from the one she'd met in Seattle. Had his and Miranda's love for each other dissipated after so many years together? Or was there something else going on?

After he left, Miranda looked as if she could cry. Sabine wrapped an arm around her shoulder, comforting her friend. Once again, Henry was left to watch his wife forlornly after Miranda stole her away. Henry seemed like a really nice guy, perhaps too nice, Lana thought. It didn't help that Sabine was so quick to abandon her husband to care for Miranda.

She hoped the baking workshop with Pierre le Monde would cheer the women up, but she had her doubts. When Lana had looked over his website, she'd been surprised at Sabine's desire to change. The reviews were mixed, and apparently the baker was known for his original and somewhat extravagant creations, not traditional recipes.

Still, she'd put the effort in to make the switch. It had taken her several tries to reach him and even more time talking him down to double his going rate. Lana certainly hoped her clients enjoyed the workshop because it was costing Dotty quite a bit to keep them satisfied.

Lana checked her watch. "Okay, guys, it's time to go meet our guide. Jane and Willow, are you coming?"

"Yes, it sounds interesting," Willow said, then looked to Jane for confirmation. Though Jane nodded, based on the set of her chin, their fight wasn't finished.

"Great," Lana said, leading her motley crew across the street.

The Jardin des Plantes was part of the vast complex of cultural activities, including a zoo, libraries, a botanical school, and museums dedicated to natural history, paleontology, mineralogy, and botany. Their guide was waiting for them by the main entrance. He was a short, unkempt man with earth under his fingernails and dirty green overalls. Lana wondered whether they had disturbed him while planting seeds.

He ushered them through the gates and into a large, open space. Rows of thick, old trees lined a path that seemed to stretch on forever. A multitude of outdoor flower beds were visible, though most were devoid of any greenery. It was still too cold for all but the hardiest varieties, Lana reckoned.

"Welcome to Jardin des Plantes. It is my honor to introduce you to our collection. These gardens were established in the seventeenth century by King Louis XIII, as a space for his doctors to grow the medicines used to treat him and his family. That is why the original name was the Royal Garden of Medicinal Plants. We now showcase four thousand five hundred specimens arranged by family and have gardens featuring plants and trees grown around the world. Our herbarium houses eight million samples of plants, making it the largest in the world."

Tamara, Sabine, and Miranda's excitement was palpable as they pointed to and then conferred about pretty much everything in sight. *They really love plants*, Lana thought. In contrast, the rest hung back, waiting to see where their guide was going to take them.

"I understand you have requested a tour of the Garden of Resource or Useful Plants," the guide said, looking to Lana for confirmation. When she nodded, he added, "Excellent choice. Please follow me."

Without further ado, the small man led them to a gorgeous art deco greenhouse close to the main entrance. "Our Garden of Resource Plants includes many of the original medicinal herbs and plants used to treat the king. Some are considered to be the oldest herbal specimens in Europe."

When he unlocked the greenhouse door, Lana was immediately captivated.

She'd had no idea medicinal plants could be so pretty. The colorful flowers and interesting-shaped leaves enchanted her. She was reaching out to touch the lacy leaf of a large shrub when Miranda swatted her hand away.

"Please do not touch the plants in this greenhouse," their guide said. "Many are poisonous, and coming in contact with any of their parts can cause rashes, headaches, or even death."

"Are you serious?" Lana gasped. She had no idea plants could be so dangerous.

"Quite," their guide replied, a peculiar smile on his lips.

"I thought you said they were medicinal."

"I did. In small doses, they have the power to heal. But if overused, they can kill or permanently damage human organs. It's a fine line. I'm certain many died before the proper dosage was determined," their guide cackled.

Lana's eyes widened. The little man was quite morbid.

"Has anyone been to the Torre Abbey Museum in Torquay, England, and visited Agatha Christie's Potent Plants garden?"

"Oh yes, we went three years ago. It was divine," Miranda gushed.

"I loved how they explained which plants Christie used to kill off characters in her books. It was quite insightful," Tamara added.

"I'm glad to hear you enjoyed it," their guide said, his eyes sparkling in delight. "It's one of my favorite holiday destinations. Our gardens are also quite unique. It will be my pleasure to introduce you to our potent plants. Before I forget, we have a wide variety of seeds for sale in the gift shop."

"I'll have to pick some up on our way out," Miranda said. "A plant would make a wonderful memento of our trip."

"That's a great idea," Angie said. "We'll have to do the same, right, Bernie?"

"Sure, doll, whatever you think will look good in our new home."

"That's right, you just moved to Seattle, didn't you?" Lana said innocently. "Why did you choose Seattle, anyway? It's quite a different climate than Florida."

Angie glanced affectionately at Bernie, cuddling close to her husband. "It's kind of a long story. We…"

"Ah, this is one of my favorites," their guide said, ruining Lana's chance to find out more about their backgrounds.

Their guide stood next to a beautiful flowering vine with gorgeous yellow blossoms that reminded Lana of a trumpet.

"Here we have the Gelsemium flower. It is a popular choice for gardeners in the southern United States and is the official flower of your state South Carolina. Its roots are used in medicines, but ingesting any part of the flower can cause dizziness, double vision, speech difficulty, muscle stiffness, paralysis, vomiting, convulsions, and death. It is a favorite weapon of Kremlin assassins because it is so fast-acting."

He admired the flowering vine before moving on to an equally beautiful plant growing next to it.

"This white flower is oleander, all parts of which are deadly." He then pointed to an evergreen tree in the corner. "That is English yew. Ingesting its leaves is usually fatal."

Lana looked up at the tree in wonder. Its needlelike leaves reminded her of rosemary. She wondered whether it was also used by any foreign organizations to kill.

"Eating English yew causes similar symptoms to belladonna, which affects the heart," he added before moving more quickly down the path winding through the many beds of trees and shrubs. "That is water hemlock, over there is white snakeroot, and that pretty plant is rosary pea. But don't be fooled; its fruit will kill you."

Lana kept her hands to herself as they moved through the vast greenhouse. She had no idea there were so many varieties that could cause so much pain and suffering.

"This attractive plant is castor bean. Its seed pods are often used in flower arrangements. Perhaps you have seen the television show *Breaking Bad*? The main character of that show used this plant's seed to kill off his competition. The processed seeds are a source of castor oil, but the beans also contain the poison ricin. It only takes eight to kill an adult. Luckily the shells are quite hard to break through. But if you do ingest it, it can cause severe vomiting, diarrhea, seizures, and even death. A Bulgarian journalist was murdered with it in 1978."

"These look really healthy," Miranda said, admiring the plant. "I have two varieties of castor bean at home, but mine aren't as robust. Do you sell the seeds for this one, as well?"

"Yes, we do. In fact, we have seeds available for all the plants that germinate."

"Excellent," Miranda said, her focus already back on the herbs and trees surrounding them.

"We should try to get several different seeds for our planned medicinal herbs garden while we are here. Wouldn't that be a nice tie-in to our vacation? And a score for Volunteer Park. I don't know of any other American herbal gardens that have strong ties to a French king, do you?" Sabine asked.

"That's an excellent point," Tamara agreed. The three horticultural enthusiasts took their time admiring the deadly plants and discussing which would make good choices for their latest project. They walked back and forth along the path of plants they had already discussed, asking their guide about germination issues. Luckily for the women, Seattle and Paris shared a similar climate, qua temperature and humidity. And the new garden they were planning in Volunteer Park included a small greenhouse. They shared photos of their current projects with their guide, all four enthusiastically trading tips and advice with each other.

After several minutes of this, the guide finally noticed that the rest were losing interest in his tour. "We're almost done with this greenhouse. Then I will walk you through the Botanical Museum before our tour ends."

As they approached the back of the greenhouse, they came upon a pretty bush with gorgeous purple flowers and black berries growing in abundance. Its branches stretched over the walkway, and several berries had fallen onto the path, as well.

"Oh, that's not good. I'll have to clean this up after we're done," their guide said, frowning at the plant's scattered fruit. He shook the branches, loosening more berries from the vine. "This is why this greenhouse is only available as a guided tour. We wouldn't want any children to accidentally eat a leaf or berry and die on us," he said, pushing several berries to the side with his shoe.

"Here's a perfect poison for Valentine's Day. It is known as belladonna, deadly nightshade, and love apple because of its ability to kill or beautify. Venetian women used drops to dilate their pupils, which made them more attractive. Some say that is why it is most often called belladonna, after the 'beautiful ladies.' Yet eating a single leaf or berry can be fatal, though it usually takes several to do any real damage."

Lana could hardly believe what she was hearing. What women did to be considered beautiful always amazed her.

"Belladonna is also used in floral arrangements. It's one of many we sell as cut flowers in our gift shop. However, it is in this greenhouse because it is also used to treat cancer patients undergoing radiation treatment, asthma, and swelling. The homeopathic cures are often considered unsafe, however, because the dosing is almost impossible to control."

Willow worked her way up to the front of the group, asking, "That is belladonna? I never knew it was so pretty."

"Do you have this plant in your garden?" Angie asked.

"No, Jane takes it for motion sickness."

"And I thought you didn't believe in pseudoscience," Angie said, her tone teasing.

"The powers of crystals are not scientifically proven, but there is quite a bit of research done into plants and their healing properties," Jane lectured.

"They just need to do more research into crystals, too. They can affect the body as much as a plant."

"Do crystals kill?" Jane asked. "Because most of the ones in this room are scientifically proven killers."

Lana reddened as Angie moved away from Jane. After yesterday's outbursts and conflicts, she was determined to keep things positive today. She couldn't let her friends bring this tour down. She looked around for Randy and found him at the back of the group, chatting with Henry. Neither one seemed to be interested in the plants. She went to her fellow guide and whispered in his ear, "Do you mind watching the group? I need to talk to Willow and Jane."

"No problem, Lana," he said, clearly honored that she trusted him with this task. She was afraid he was going to salute her.

Lana grabbed her friends' arms and pulled them back down the path they had come from. "Ladies, I love you, but this has to stop. Who cares if Angie believes in crystals? What does it matter?"

Jane blushed and looked to the ground. "I shouldn't have jumped down her throat. I guess I'm still reeling from Chad's comments," she admitted.

Lana was so glad she hadn't told Jane or Willow about her brief affair with Chad. They would have been extremely disappointed in her.

"Yesterday you two were getting along so well. I am going to ask you again to forget about babies for the rest of the tour. You'll have plenty of time to fight about them after you get home, okay?"

Jane and Willow glared at each other, but neither made a move.

"I'm really worried about you two," Lana said, her tone softening. She took their hands and held them close together. Willow hesitantly took Jane's. Moments later, Jane intertwined her fingers through her wife's.

"Sorry, Lana," Jane said.

"You really should apologize to Angie," Lana added.

Jane nodded. "I will."

Lana looked at her friends, both with their heads hung low. She put an arm around each shoulder. "Excellent. Now, lovebirds, what do you think of the plants tour?"

"Umm, it's not really my thing, but the others seem to be loving it," Willow said.

"They really do know a lot about poisonous plants. I don't know if I want to visit their new garden," Jane added, getting a chuckle out of them both.

Lana glanced back up the path and saw that their guide had reached the end of the medicinal herbs greenhouse.

"Oops, we'd better catch up. Well, I should anyway. You two take your time," Lana said as she hustled to catch up to her group.

18

Kicked Out of the Moulin Rouge

February 15—Day Four of the Wanderlust Tour in Paris, France

Lana woke up on February 15, wishing her memories of last night's events were only a horrible dream. Unfortunately, when she saw her blouse covered in red wine, she knew they were not. Her group really had gotten kicked out of the Moulin Rouge on Valentine's Day.

What had started out as an entertaining evening ended up a nightmare. The show was quite exhilarating and not as risqué as she had feared. Her guests seemed to be enjoying themselves, laughing at the jokes and clapping along in time with the lively music. Things were going really well, until Chad, already drunk from the preceding champagne tasting, said something inappropriate to Edward about how good Tamara looked in lingerie. Lana was certain it was Chad's way of getting back at Edward for insulting his pride during that silly boat race. Still, their tiff didn't warrant Chad telling Edward about how Tamara worked her way through college by dancing at a local strip club.

Her husband defended his wife's honor, knocking Chad into a neighboring table. While the dancers on stage performed their famous can-can routine, her guests began brawling with the neighboring tables, in time with the lively music. Wine, champagne, and breadsticks flew through the air. The police soon arrived, and several patrons were hauled away to cool off for the night—including Edward and Chad.

Lana was incredibly mortified by her guests' behavior. After conferring with Randy and Dotty, her boss authorized Lana to kick both men off the tour, if need be. Lana felt horrible having to ask Dotty about this possibility, but enough was enough. If the two men couldn't find a way to get along, one or both had to go. She only hoped that without so much alcohol flowing through their bodies, they would both be more reasonable. Their group had to get through three more days of tours together. She doubted anyone would be leaving five stars for this trip.

That morning, when she entered the breakfast room, Sabine and Henry were already sitting at one table, feeding each other eggs. They were so cute together, she almost felt bad for Henry that the other two couples were there. Sabine did tend to forget about her husband when Miranda and Tamara were around. Those two women sat a table close by, deep in conversation. Lana wasn't certain when their husbands would be released from jail. Calling the police was on her morning's to-do list.

Angie and Bernie were glowing with positive energy. They had had a wonderful time at their rub-in and had discovered two new recipes, to boot. Willow and Jane were also in a loving mood, Lana was happy to see. The restaurant they had dined at was quite romantic and the food superb. Lana was glad some of her guests had a wonderful Valentine's Day.

Just as everyone was getting settled into their breakfasts, Chad and Edward walked into the dining room. Both looked worse for the wear, with a thick layer of stubble on their chins, and reeked of alcohol.

Lana rose to greet them, hoping they would both be in reasonable moods after a night in a jail cell. Randy must have had the same thought, for he stood up and placed himself between the men and their wives. "How are you doing today, gentlemen?" he asked.

Edward walked around Randy and straight to his wife. She began to rise. "Don't bother getting up. I've booked a ticket back to Seattle. You are not welcome to join me. I'll have your things boxed up by the time you get back."

Tamara laid a hand on her husband's arm. "Edward, I was in college. It was years before we met. I bet you've done stupid things you haven't mentioned to me before."

Edward laughed. "Nope, I've told you everything. And it's not like you got drunk at a party once and mooned someone. You were a stripper for years and you didn't think to mention it? What other secrets are you hiding from me?"

Tamara put her head in her hands and began to shake. Edward looked at his wife. There was no love left in his eyes. He started to walk away, then turned back to her. "Oh, and I've blocked your credit cards. Try earning your own money for a change."

Chad began to cackle. *What a horrible man*, Lana thought.

Tamara's head whipped up. "You had no right to tell him, Chad!"

Chad shrugged. "You should have been honest."

Tamara stood up and stormed out of the room. Unfazed by her show of emotion, Chad walked to the breakfast buffet and began filling his plate.

Sabine leaned over to Miranda. "Did they date in college?"

"I don't think so," she answered, a puzzled frown on her face.

As Lana watched her guests storming off in all directions, she wanted to curl up in a ball and give up. This was officially the tour from hell. Instead of throwing in the towel, she went to the lobby in search of Tamara, finding her in the bar with a bloody Mary before her. Her guest took a large swig before announcing, "Miranda will never believe that Chad and I weren't intimate. It's probably better if I leave. I'll book a ticket in a few minutes."

"Are you and Chad romantically involved?" Lana asked, knowing she was overstepping her bounds, but needing to know how bad this situation was. If Tamara and Chad were having an affair, Lana was going to cancel the trip. Otherwise, the guests would probably murder each other before the week was over.

"No, though he's tried. Chad isn't exactly faithful," Tamara said, before raising the drink to her lips again.

"Why does Miranda stay with him?"

"Money, honey."

"What? That's crazy!"

"Heck, who am I to talk. I don't know why I'm still married to Eddie.

We used to do everything together like partners should, but now he's more interested in his smartphone and chitchatting with colleagues than me." Tamara swigged another gulp, then turned to Lana, her face filled with anger.

"If Edward hadn't been helping me with my business, I probably would have left him years ago. Thanks to Chad, I've not only lost my husband and home, but I'm also going to have to file for bankruptcy. Edward was about to bail me out again. Things haven't been going well financially."

Tamara polished off her drink and signaled for another. Lana felt bad for taking advantage of her guest's increasingly inebriated state, but this was her chance to find out more about Tamara's friends.

"Who is Daniel?"

"Chad's younger brother. He had some sort of chest infection and died quite unexpectedly. Miranda said Chad hasn't been the same since."

"Why did she get so upset about Chad opening a restaurant?"

"Wouldn't you, if your husband made a major life decision and didn't tell you about it?" Tamara smiled at the bartender as he set another drink in front of her.

As if called, Miranda walked into the bar and crossed over to her friend. Tamara stiffened, but Miranda pulled her into a hug. "I am so sorry about Edward. Chad can be such a brute, especially when he's drinking. He told me you two never slept together. Once Edward gets that through his thick skull, he'll come around. It's his male pride that drove him back to Seattle."

"Our grandparents were neighbors. If Chad hadn't have gone to the club for a stag party, he never would have known what I did." Miranda let out a peculiar laugh. "You know, it was such a shock to meet your husband all those years ago, and to discover it was Chad, of all people. I've wanted to tell you about it for ages, but I didn't want Edward to find out."

Miranda stroked her hair. "It's okay. You didn't do anything wrong."

Tamara snorted. "Try telling that to Edward."

"Ladies, I hate to interrupt, but I think it's better for everyone if Chad leaves the tour," Lana said, wanting to resolve this current crisis.

"No! You can't do that. I need this time to work out a few issues with him. Please don't ask him to leave," Miranda pleaded. Lana was shocked. She could hardly imagine that Miranda would want Chad to stay, considering how badly he had behaved.

"Look, Chad's not himself right now. We're dealing with a few personal problems, not very well, I might add. But I need to be with him right now. If you ask him to leave, my marriage will be over."

Lana bit her tongue until she tasted blood. She wanted to ask why Miranda would want to stay with him, though she knew it was all about the money. "I'm sorry, but I have to think of the others. I can imagine Tamara won't be comfortable around him, and I know he's angered Bernie. Everyone on the trip deserves to have a good time, and frankly, when Chad is around, everyone is tense."

Miranda grabbed her hands. "Lana, I am begging you. My marriage depends on him coming to the picnic. He wants to judge the food we make during the workshop. I know it sounds silly, but Chad's ego needs this. If he feels valued, he'll lighten up. He hasn't told anyone yet, but he had a business deal fall through last month. And the *Seattle Chronicle* dropped his column, as well. He's feeling unappreciated, and that disagreement with Bernie at the market made things worse. We've been through this kind of thing before, and he always comes around."

What a bizarre relationship, Lana thought. Then again, if Chad lost his brother and a major business deal within a short span of time, that could explain his odd behavior. Though why critiquing food made by a group of amateurs was so important to him was beyond Lana. She was glad her husband had the decency to divorce her when he found another, instead of playing these head games with her. Being single was infinitely better than feeling trapped in a bad marriage.

"Tamara, what do you think?"

"I would rather Chad not join us at the baking workshop. I need some time away from him. The picnic isn't until this afternoon, right?"

Miranda nodded enthusiastically. "That sounds like a great idea. I'm sure he won't mind."

"Okay," Lana conceded. "He can stay for now. But if there are any other incidents, I'm going to have to ask him to leave."

"No problem, Lana. Things will be better after the picnic, I promise."

19

Baking a Baguette

"Kneading the dough does not mean simply pushing it around the bowl. You're activating the yeasts, which allows the dough to rise into the traditional baguette you all desire. You have to massage it, not punch at it," Pierre le Monde growled.

His snappiness was starting to get on Lana's nerves. When Sabine had raved about what a great teacher he was, Lana had expected a more relaxed, even jovial baker who was good with clients. Pierre was the opposite.

Her group was gathered around a stainless steel countertop in le Monde's baking school. In the center stood all the ingredients they used to mix their own balls of dough. Their bowls were so close together, they had to take turn mixing, for fear of otherwise knocking over the other person's work.

Pierre stood behind Tamara, holding her hands while helping her practice the proper technique. Tamara seemed to be unfamiliar with a kitchen, confused as to how mixers worked, and unsure what a spatula was called. When Pierre said they were to use the food processors to mix their tapenades, she had to ask which kitchen appliance he meant.

She must have a cook or eat out all the time, Lana thought.

Pierre watched Tamara work her dough, frowning. "Give it more oomph! It is not a delicate flower; you have to really knead if you want it to rise properly."

Lana liked to cook but had never taken a baking workshop before. So far, she was not impressed by Pierre's rather abrupt style and almost arrogant manner of speaking.

Most of her guests didn't seem to mind. Angie and Bernie were having the time of their lives. They spent most of the first hour throwing flour at each other, making silly shapes with their dough, tasting every ingredient, and chatting easily with Pierre about their favorite recipes.

Sabine and Miranda were also loving every second. Henry worked quietly next to his wife, smiling at their jokes, but not really participating in the merriment. The same could be said of Willow and Jane, though they did seem to be enjoying themselves.

After checking everyone's progress, Pierre began pulling small bowls filled with a variety of ingredients out of a cooler and placing them in the middle of the table. "If you wish to add any of the rosemary, garlic, olives, dried nuts, berries, or cheeses to your loaf, you can do so before we get it ready for the oven. While the bread is baking, we will also make a selection of tapenades and dips. This is your chance to experiment with new tastes and creations. I will show you how to prepare a few basic recipes, then I want you to use your fantasy."

"I like this guy," Bernie said to his wife.

Angie giggled in agreement. "It's more fun than I expected."

After Pierre approved their dough, he showed them how to ball it up, then grabbed a tray and began laying their creations on it.

"The last and perhaps most important step is allowing the dough time to ferment and rise. It takes two to three hours before it is ready to bake."

Lana looked at her watch, stricken. It had taken an hour just to get this far. Considering the workshop was only three hours long, they wouldn't have time to actually bake the bread at this rate. And they still had to make the tapenades and dips to go with it.

Pierre must have noticed her reaction, because he added, "Don't worry, this usually happens. I have dough already prepared for you. At least you now know how to mix the ingredients and knead it properly. Let me get the dough, then we will move on to the most important part of the process—shaping the loaf."

Tamara laughed. "We better not tell Chad that we didn't actually make the·dough. He's staking his reputation as The Fussy Gourmet on being able to tell the difference between our baguettes."

Miranda looked as if she might cry. "Oh, no. You're right. Here I thought we were helping him feel appreciated again. His ego is so bruised right now. Darn it." She punched her dough ball, then wiped away a tear. "I just don't know what else to do."

Pierre erupted, "The Fussy Gourmet is on your tour?" He looked as if he could throttle someone.

The kitchen went silent as the students exchanged perplexed glances. Finally Lana spoke up, "Yes, he is. Is there a problem?"

"That man is pure evil!" Pierre shouted. "He ruined my restaurant with his horrible review. That traditionalist doesn't understand the modern kitchen. No one would risk investing in my chain after he tore apart my menu. That's why I'm back here, giving these stupid workshops to tourists." Pierre looked so dejected. He leaned heavily against the wall. "I want you to leave."

Lana couldn't believe it. What horrible luck! Worse yet, Bernie and Angie's fears were justified. Chad was, in fact, capable of destroying their dreams. She looked to them and saw they had both gone as white as sheets.

When no one moved, Pierre yelled, "Get out of my bakery!"

"There must be some sort of mix-up –" Lana said in a soothing voice, completely unsure of what to do next.

Pierre stood up, his eyes watering, and pointed to the door. Before Lana could react, Randy stepped in. "Whatever happened in the past, The Fussy Gourmet isn't actually in this room. But the rest of the tour guests are, and they have paid royally for the privilege of learning from you. Wouldn't the best revenge be blowing his socks off with your wonderful bread?"

Randy was so calm and rational. Lana was in awe. Better yet, his reasoning got through to the baker.

Pierre nodded slowly. "Is The Fussy Gourmet going to taste all of the food we make?"

"Yes, he will be judging the breads and dips," Randy said.

Pierre's grin seemed almost evil. "Let me get the dough."

20

Picnicking under the Eiffel Tower

After Lana got her guests back to the hotel, she used most of her hour break getting ready for the picnic. They had purchased quite a few sausages and cheeses at the market to go along with the dips and bread they had made today. Lana was quite glad Randy was there to help carry all of their supplies. Between the plates, silverware, drinks, food, and blankets, they had three large bags to lug to the park.

The taxi dropped them off at the Champs de Mars, a vast park situated between the École Militaire, where Napoleon had trained to be a soldier, and the Eiffel Tower. At one end was the Wall for Peace monument, made up of several large gray columns and glass walls etched with messages calling for peace on earth. But the highlight was the slender monument towering above them. From this distance, it was easy to see the many segments of the metal skeleton holding Gustave Eiffel's masterpiece together. At three hundred meters high, it had been the tallest building in the world when it was constructed in 1889. Lana was glad to see the skies were clear. After their picnic, her group would climb up the tower, and the views from both platforms were supposed to be phenomenal.

While she and Randy got everything set up, the guests strolled around the park, taking pictures of the tower and each other. Luckily the sun had warmed the earth up a bit. It was still on the cold side, but Lana understood why Dotty wanted to include it on their romantic trip. *It's quite special, picnicking here underneath the Eiffel Tower*, Lana thought.

It was only too bad Chad was here, as well. Perhaps this was her payback for having lied to him about her profession, she thought, resolving to never lie again to a potential suitor. Simply setting the food out on their blanket reminded her too much of their picnic and last date at Gas Works Park. Lana looked to Chad and Miranda, walking side by side, yet not speaking to each other. He was not at all the man she thought he was. Luckily, they hadn't dated long enough for this incident to break her spirit. Chad was a speed bump, not a dead end sign, on her path to finding true love.

In addition to all the food that the tour was providing, Sabine had bought a cheesecake from a shop next to their hotel, and Miranda had picked up berries to go with it. *As if we needed more to eat*, Lana thought, wondering whether they would be able to finish even half of the dips and tapenades they had made this morning. Not to mention the eight baguettes, all topped with rich ingredients, as well as the cheeses and meats she picked up at the market. Lana doubted she would need to eat dinner tonight.

When a cool gust of wind blew away several napkins, Randy asked, "I'm not trying to knock the itinerary, but why are we having a picnic? Technically, it's still winter."

Lana laughed. "Dotty always says that picnicking under the Eiffel Tower was one of the most romantic things she did in Paris with her late husband."

"Were they here in February?"

"Probably not. But you have to admit, the view is quite romantic."

Randy gazed up at the tower. "I bet my girlfriend would agree with you."

"Your girlfriend?" Lana sputtered. She'd never considered that he was with someone.

"Gloria and I met while working as mountaineer guides."

"Oh, well, at least she understands your schedule."

"Frankly, I think she's jealous of me being to travel internationally. I wouldn't be surprised if she wants to apply at Wanderlust after I get back. At least..." Randy looked away in embarrassment. "Most tours aren't as chaotic as this one, are they?" he asked.

Lana considered his question. "This tour is definitely the exception, but travel does tend to amplify any existing fractures in our guests' relationships. But most of the clients I've worked with so far were able to set aside any problems and enjoy themselves, far more easily than this bunch is able to."

Randy nodded, chuckling. "It's the same with mountaineering. You get these groups of computer geeks who've never climbed a hill before, yet seem to think they can scale Rainier in an afternoon. We spend weeks training, but most of them don't really listen. Instead they egg each other on about who's going to reach the top first. Inevitably, once we hit that first crevice and they have to use their newly learned skills instead of their muscles, the stress levels soar."

Before Lana could respond, Bernie returned.

"I am starving," Bernie said while rubbing his belly. "I can't wait to dig in." He sat cross-legged on one side of the blanket, patting the space next to him for his wife.

"Grab a plate and dig in," Lana said, handing Bernie silverware.

"Oh, this looks to die for!" Angie exclaimed, grabbing a chunk of cheese as she sat.

"Could we start with the cheesecake?" Sabine asked as she and her friends approached the blanket. "The chocolate sauce should still be warm." The hotel's restaurant had heated it up and packed it in a thermos-like container for her right before they left. "I can serve it, if you like?"

"That would be lovely," Lana said, handing her a stack of plates. "Thanks, Sabine."

"Let me help," Miranda said, sitting next to her friend. "Where are the berries, Lana? Oh wait, I see them." She grabbed the small paper bag filled with raspberries and blueberries she had bought from a fruit stand close to the hotel.

The two women worked quickly. Miranda handed the plates to Lana, who passed them around to her guests. When it was Chad's turn, Miranda said, "Wait just a second." She stuck her hand in the paper bag and quickly added another handful of fruit to his plate before Sabine poured chocolate sauce over it. "Extra berries, just the way you like it. Right, Chad?"

He nodded with a smile as he accepted his plate. To Lana's relief, he was quiet, seeming to understand that he had crossed a line yesterday. The last thing she needed was for him to start another argument. They weren't out of the woods quite yet, though; they still had to get through the taste testing. Lana looked to Bernie, fervently hoping that the Floridian wouldn't pester Chad today. They all deserved a chance to enjoy the afternoon, tension-free.

Once all the guests were served, Lana took a bite of her cheesecake and let it melt in her mouth. It was always one of her favorite desserts. This one was lighter than those she was used to eating in the States and slightly more bitter. The crust was not crumbly, but thick and buttery. She had never topped it with warm chocolate sauce before but would be doing so again. It was scrumptious. The fruit was a nice touch; the combination of sweet and sour made it even more delicious.

Lana hasn't eaten so decadently in all of her life, as she had on this trip. The French foods and desserts were incredibly rich, and the combinations of sauces and herbs were a delight for her taste buds. She was certain that her waistline was expanding with every bite.

Miranda took a bite of hers. "Yum. This reminds me of our first date in that little café in downtown Pullman. We shared a piece of cheesecake, do you remember?"

When Chad gazed at his wife, Lana swore she saw tears in his eyes. "Gino's. Yes, I remember. You were so excited about a role you'd gotten in *Grease*. That night, you told me that you were going to apply to that acting school in New York."

Miranda nodded, "That's true. I'd forgotten about that; I never did get up the nerve to actually apply to The Juilliard School." She sighed, recalling that fateful night. "And you were going to be a restaurateur. You sketched out your dream restaurant on a napkin for me that night. I still have it," she chuckled.

Chad put down his plate. "What happened to us, Miranda? Where did it all go wrong?"

Miranda, put her hand on his leg. "We're not broken yet. We just need a recharge, that's all."

Chad looked away as a single tear rolled down his cheek.

Lana felt so embarrassed. They needed therapy, not a vacation. The stress of travel was making whatever crisis they were going through so much worse.

Hoping to divert her guests' attention from the couple in crisis, Lana took her last bite and said cheerily, "That was delicious. Thank you so much, Sabine."

"Can I have some of this tea?" Angie pointed at the two thermoses in the center of the picnic blanket. "I am simply parched from our walk."

"Of course! We have fresh orange juice and tea. Miranda was kind enough to brew up two kinds of herbal infusions. Does anyone else want a cup to help to warm up?" She held up the two thermoses. "What did you make for us, Miranda?"

"Oh, the smaller one is Chad's hibiscus tea. It helps reduce blood pressure and cholesterol. The other one is a green tea, with mint, stinging nettle leaf, ginger, and cinnamon mixed in. I picked up the herbs at the Jardin des Plantes gift shop."

"That mix sounds wonderful," Willow said, holding out a cup.

"I want to try Chad's tea," Bernie said. Angie shook her head. Was she forbidding Bernie from drinking the same tea as Chad, or was she upset that he was trying to engage the food critic again? Lana couldn't tell.

"Go ahead, but it's rather tart, and I forgot the honey," Miranda said.

Chad grabbed the hibiscus tea and poured a large cup, then set the thermos next to him, out of Bernie's reach. Bernie started to lean over, but Angie glared at her husband, making clear that he was to leave it be.

Chad smirked, then downed his drink and poured himself another. "It's perfect, Miranda, thanks."

She smiled at him serenely. "Anything for you."

Chad squeezed her hand but didn't meet her eyes.

It took her group quite a while to finish their cake, partly because it was so yummy, and partly because everyone seemed to be getting along again. Her guests joked and teased each other, while Henry and Bernie held their wives tight. Miranda moved closer to Chad and tried to cuddle, but he pulled away from her clunky attempts, laying his hand over hers instead.

After everyone finished their cake, Randy collected the plates while Lana opened up the picnic basket full of bread. "So, should we dig in, or do we let the taste tester sample our creations first?" Lana asked the group. She still didn't feel comfortable addressing Chad directly.

"The Fussy Gourmet is going to judge our baguettes, right? Then he should sample them first," Bernie stated. He was strangely excited about Chad's opinions of their culinary efforts. Lana wondered whether it was because Bernie thought Chad would choose his baguette as the best, or whether he was simply trying to get back onto Chad's good side before he opened his new restaurant.

Either way, Lana doubted Chad would appreciate Bernie's baguette. According to Pierre le Monde, baguettes were usually not filled, but another sort of French bread called a *fougasse* was. However, seeing as Chad was going to sample everything, Pierre encouraged his guests to be liberal with the toppings and fillings.

Only Miranda had resisted, leaving hers plain. Most of the others had topped their loaves with fresh herbs, spices, and cheeses, except Bernie, who had filled his with figs and dried berries. Given Chad's reaction to fusion food at the market, he was almost certainly too obsessed with the purity of French food to enjoy any baguette but Miranda's.

"I'm game," Chad said, pulling out his trusty notebook before throwing back some more tea. He set the cup down and closed his eyes. "Phew. I don't know if it's the cold wind or the hot tea, but I feel like I'm burning up."

Miranda felt his forehead. "Oh, no, you must be coming down with a cold. And this cool breeze isn't helping. Eating may make you feel better, or at least give you more energy."

Chad nodded and took hold of the first baguette. He cut off the end, then a second slice, and popped that into his mouth. "Too much sea salt. A little goes a long way, folks," he stated before pulling a second loaf out of the basket. "Wow, olives belong in the tapenade, not baked into the bread," he said, chewing slowly.

When he took out the third, he stared at the lumpy loaf before laying it down and cutting off a slice. He held the piece in his hand and frowned at it. "Someone confused a *fougasse* for a baguette." He looked to Bernie. "I think

I'll skip yours."

"What's wrong? Are you afraid your palate will be ruined by my exquisite creation?"

Chad laughed. "I'm more concerned that it'll give me indigestion."

"Some food critic. He doesn't even taste the food he's supposed to be judging," Bernie said to the rest, clearly taunting Chad. "I wonder what your *Seattle Chronicle* readers will think."

Chad rose to the bait and nibbled on one edge. "That is the worst baguette I have ever sampled. Happy?"

"Fine, more for us." Bernie grabbed the piece out of Chad's hand and popped it into his mouth.

Chad sniggered as Bernie grimaced, then spit his bread into his napkin. "Fig was not the right choice," he mumbled to Angie.

His wife tore off a chunk. "I don't know, it's got potential," she said.

Chad poured himself another cup of tea, washing his mouth out. He took the next loaf out of the basket and stared at its texture. "It's like someone baked a map onto the bread."

Miranda smirked. "Sure, the cracks do resemble roads, I guess."

Chad began cutting off a slice as a bird flew low over their blanket, eyeing the food. "Did you see that? He waved at me."

"What did you say, honey?" Miranda asked.

"That crow waved hello."

Miranda and Sabine exchanged glances. "Really? If you say so," Miranda said, concern in her voice.

Lana was beginning to grow uneasy, too. "Maybe we should pack everything up and get warmed up," she said. She didn't want her guests to get sick because of this picnic. It was sunnier than back in Seattle, but still not warm.

"No, I'm fine," Chad said. "I promised, Miranda. It's the least I can do," he said and grabbed another loaf. This time he tore a chunk off with his teeth. "The garlic is just right. Well done."

Angie blushed with pride but said nothing.

Chad bit off another piece and chewed it slowly, with his mouth open.

What is wrong with him? Lana wondered. It was irritating to watch.

"Does he always eat like this when he's reviewing food?" Tamara asked Miranda in a whisper.

"I don't know, he eats alone when he's reviewing a place for his column," Miranda murmured back.

An ant crawled over Chad's pant leg. "I love you," he told it, as the insect continued marching towards the dips.

"Hon, are you okay?" Miranda asked.

"Sure, never been better," Chad said.

"Did our quartz give him hallucinations?" Angie asked her husband. "I really didn't think he'd have put it under his pillow."

Bernie shrugged. "I don't know what's going on with him. Maybe he went to a bar when we were baking."

Chad tore off another piece of Angie's garlic baguette and dipped it into the tapenade closest to him. It was Jane's dried berry and yogurt concoction. "Yum, who made this one?" he asked.

Jane said nothing, but Willow shone with pride. "My wife did."

Chad looked at Jane with a loopy grin. Jane turned her head away, before whipping back to face him, staring at Chad.

"Chad? Are you feeling dizzy or light-headed?" Jane asked.

Lana noticed that her tone was suddenly professional and she was trying to make eye contact with him.

"What are those firemen doing on the tower?" Chad asked, his mouth full of bread.

Lana looked to the Eiffel Tower, but saw no firemen. When she turned back, Chad collapsed onto the blanket, his body convulsing. A chunk of baguette fell out of his mouth as he twisted and turned, knocking over the dips and drinks spread out on it.

"Chad! No!" Miranda screamed, throwing herself on her husband, attempting to stop him from moving. "What's happening?"

"Stand back, give him space," Jane yelled. "Lana, call an ambulance."

Jane pushed Miranda aside and grabbed Chad's head, holding it steady while she lifted his eyelid. "His pupils are dilated." She felt for his pulse. "It's quite erratic. I think he's been poisoned."

Lana dialed 911, before remembering the emergency services number in Europe was 112. "We need an ambulance at the Champs de Mars. A man is dying!"

Jane tilted his head to the side and stuck her fingers down his throat, trying to force him to throw up. He began convulsing so badly, she had trouble holding him down. Randy tried to help, but Chad was quite strong. By the time Jane got her fingers back into his mouth, Chad stopped moving. Her efforts produced no results.

Jane stepped back to let Miranda be close to him. Chad's ragged breathing was barely audible. Miranda lay over him, weeping softly. "My love," she whispered.

Her girlfriends stood behind her, holding each other tight.

21

The Baker Killed My Husband!

By the time ambulance and police cars tore over the Champs de Mars, it was too late. Chad was gone.

Sabine and Tamara had to pry Miranda off of her husband to allow the paramedics access to him.

"What happened?" one asked as she checked Chad's body for vital signs. There were none.

"It may have been food poisoning. His eyes were dilated, and he was hallucinating just before he went into convulsions," Jane explained.

"And you are?" asked a police officer.

"A doctor. Jane Jeffries." She held out her hand for the officer.

"That baker killed him! He knew Chad would be judging our baguettes. He must have poisoned the dough!" Miranda cried.

Lana looked over the remnants of their picnic, now tipped and turned over on the blanket. Could their baguettes really be the murder weapon? Or was Miranda's grief making her say crazy things?

Lana's heart went out to the woman. No matter how rocky their relationship was, it was surely horrible to see your husband die in front of you.

A second officer stepped forward, older than the first. "I am Inspector Boucher. Is this your husband?" he asked Miranda.

"Yes, Chad Dumfrey. We've been married thirty-six years." She began weeping again.

"My condolences, madame. I will need to take your statement. You will want to accompany us to the morgue, *non?*"

Miranda bobbed her head in affirmation.

"I'm coming with you," Sabine said resolutely.

Miranda squeezed her hand as Henry whispered into his wife's ear, "Is that a good idea?"

"Miranda needs me."

"She always needs you. Maybe this time, a lawyer would be better."

Sabine shook her head and hugged her girlfriend tight.

The French inspector conferred with the paramedics before addressing Lana's group. "I am going to need to take statements from everyone in your group. But first, who is this baker?" Boucher took a small notebook and pen out of his pocket.

"Pierre le Monde! He hated my husband and knew Chad was going to taste all of the food first."

"Why would a French baker want to kill your husband?"

"Because Chad gave his business a bad review. Le Monde told us he had opened a patisserie a few years ago in Seattle. He was in the process of turning it into a chain when Chad's review convinced the investors to back out. Le Monde hates my husband, and now he's gotten his revenge," Miranda wailed. She was inconsolable.

The investigator took her accusations seriously, writing down Miranda's words in his notebook. Lana's brow furrowed. Le Monde had told them during the workshop that Chad's review destroyed his dreams, but was it really true? Or was there another reason the patisserie ended up going bankrupt?

While the police photographed the scene, the inspector took their statements, asking about the day's events and anything strange they may have seen. Too soon, the paramedics were wheeling Chad's body away, with Miranda and Sabine trailing close behind.

As the police began clearing the site, Lana tapped the lead officer on the shoulder. The remnants of their picnic were still strewn across the blanket and grass. It was a colorful mess of dips, baguettes, and herbal teas. "What about the picnic stuff? Should I throw it away?"

"No, my officers will bag it as evidence. Our lab will want to test it all, in case Mr. Dumfrey was indeed poisoned."

Lana stared at the simple loaves of bread and gulped. If the baguettes were the murder weapon, then, in a way, that would make her party to the murder. She was the one who had arranged for them to take a workshop with Pierre le Monde.

22

Death by Baguette?

"Death by baguette? You have got to be joking," Dotty said, her tone serious.

"I'm afraid not. Jane is fairly certain that he was poisoned. The police will know what killed him soon enough. The officer in charge said they were making Chad's autopsy a priority."

"Who would do such a thing?"

"His wife thinks it was the baker. Apparently Chad wrote a terrible review of his patisserie, and the man blamed him for its failure."

"Can one review really ruin a place?" Dotty mused aloud.

"That's a great question, Dotty. Angie and Bernie seem to think so. But Seattle isn't New York. There aren't Michelin-starred restaurants opening every week. And the *Seattle Chronicle* isn't exactly the *New York Times*."

"How is the wife holding up?"

"Miranda is in shock. Luckily, her two best friends are here so she wants to stay. Besides, they won't release Chad's body until they have finished the autopsy. Jane said it will take longer because of the toxicology reports and because this is a suspicious death."

"What a horrible way to celebrate Valentine's Day."

"The worst," Lana agreed emphatically.

"What about the others' husbands? This is a couples' tour. Do you think Miranda being alone and grieving is going to cause trouble within the group?"

Lana inhaled deeply, knowing it was time to come clean. "I haven't been honest with you, Dotty. I think all of the marriages need a jump start and most of our guests are not romantically inclined. One husband already left the tour after a horrid fight with his wife. I don't know if it's the group dynamics or the lovers theme that's causing the tension, but this has not been a very relaxing vacation for any of our guests."

"I am truly sorry to hear that. This happened on last year's tour, as well. One of the husbands pushed another into the Seine because he was ogling his wife. Maybe the whole theme puts too much pressure on our guests to be the perfect romantic couple for an entire week. Which, if you ask me, is unrealistic, no matter how wonderful a relationship is. I might have to reconsider offering this tour again. I sure hope no one asks for a refund." Dotty paused a moment, processing the bad news. "Are Willow and Jane getting along at least?"

"They are up and down right now. Every time I think they're doing alright, something sets off another argument."

"Oh, no. I hoped that this trip would be their chance to get through this impasse. I guess I don't need to start knitting baby sweaters quite yet."

"Not just yet, I'm afraid. Until one or both are willing to compromise, there won't be any pitter-patter of tiny feet in their house."

Dotty was silent a moment. "Can you tell me anything positive about your trip?"

Lana thought hard. "The weather's been remarkably warm, and Paris is even more beautiful than I expected, especially once you walk around the city center."

"Well, that's something. How are the other two guests handling Chad's death?"

"Bernie and Angie are quite emotional, actually. Watching Chad die really hit them hard."

"I can imagine! It sounds positively horrifying to see someone die like that. Oh, Lana, I didn't even ask how you are holding up."

Lana considered Dotty's question. The truth was, she felt absolutely nothing. Chad had lied to her and treated most of the people on this tour pretty horribly. As disturbing as it was to see another person die, the fact that it was Chad left her cold. "I'm doing okay," she conceded. "I didn't know him well, so it makes it easier to keep my distance from it. It was a pretty awful way to die, though."

"Have the police gotten in touch?"

"They have the baker in custody, but it's too soon to know if he was truly involved. The lead investigator said he would let me know if there were any new developments. He also took a copy of our itinerary so he can find us, if need be."

"Could you keep me informed, as well?"

"I will."

"Say, what are your afternoon plans?"

"Since no one wanted to climb the Eiffel Tower after the police released us, I canceled the afternoon tour and am going to join Jane and Willow for a late lunch. They didn't get to know Chad very well, either, and aren't too fazed by it."

"That sounds nice. I hope you can turn this into a lovely evening."

"We will do our best. Talk to you soon, Dotty."

* * *

Lana knocked tentatively on Jane's door, hoping her friends were both in a good mood. She could find Randy and have dinner with him, if they were quibbling again. Lana only hoped they'd asked her to join them because they wanted to hang out, not to have her mediate their conversations.

When Willow opened the door, she looked radiant in her yellow strapless sundress. Jane was also dolled up in a stunning black dress that showed off her figure. Lana had never seen Jane wear anything form-fitting. "Oh, my! You two look gorgeous. Are you sure you want me tagging along?"

"Of course," Jane said, wrapping her arm around Willow's waist. "We have you to thank for helping us find each other again."

"It's Paris and Dotty that made that happen, not me," Lana said, smiling at the two.

"We saw a bistro a few streets away that looks really cute. Should we try it?" Willow asked.

"That sounds great!"

The three friends soon found themselves being shown to a cozy table next to the window of a tiny corner café. On one side was a glass case filled with sumptuous-looking delicacies. The rest of the space was filled with round tables covered in checkered tablecloths. The view out the window was also pleasant. The bistro was situated on a busy street, and Lana enjoyed watching the people and animals pass by.

Her friends sat next to each other, giggling like schoolgirls while making silly comments about some of the high fashion popular in Paris. Lana stared in amazement. They were giddy with love. It was wonderfully refreshing to see them back to normal.

"So, not to be a jerk, but what happened to make you two be so nice to each other again?"

"I guess Chad's death reminded us of how short life is and how we need to enjoy it to the fullest," Jane said, leaning against Willow.

"Because the bottom line is, baby or not, we want to stay together," Willow said, grasping her partner's hand.

"You two just made my day. And Dotty's, too. She's pretty worried about both of you."

"I know that's why she suggested we join this tour," Willow confirmed.

"And I'm so glad you surprised me with the trip," Jane conceded. "I never would have agreed to it, if you had asked first. Since opening my practice, I've gotten to know my patients' needs so well, they feel like family. It's hard to step back and trust that another doctor could take as good care of them. But those other doctors trust me with their patients. I have to show them the same respect."

"Is that why you've been so resistant to taking on a partner?"

Jane nodded. "I'm afraid so. Silly, I know. We've all taken the same courses and vow to save lives. Heck, I went to medical school with most of those who want to work with me and would trust them implicitly with my own life. This trip has really helped remind me that asking for help is not a sign of weakness. I don't have to do it all on my own."

"Of course you don't," Willow murmured.

Lana's heart soared with joy, grateful that Chad's death was good for something.

Moments later, their waiter set a basket of bread on the table and handed them all menus. When he described the *menu du jour*, Lana's stomach began to rumble in anticipation. They all ordered the recommended daily special— a plate of shredded pork, mixed vegetables, and new potatoes with roasted almonds.

After the waiter poured them a glass of red wine and retreated to the kitchen, Willow grimaced at the mini-baguettes and winked at Lana. "I think I'll pass on the bread," she whispered. Her eyes sparkled as she asked, "So not to be morbid, but do you really think the baker killed Chad?"

Lana frowned. "It is one heck of a coincidence that we were taking a workshop with a man Chad had wronged. I wonder if Miranda or Sabine knew."

"What do you mean?" Willow asked.

"Sabine specifically requested that we take a workshop led by Pierre. Friends of hers were raving about what a great teacher he is."

Willow snorted. "I don't know why her friends were so enthusiastic; the man is a horrible instructor! He seemed more interested in rubbing up against Tamara than actually teaching the class."

"He was snappy with everyone," Jane added.

"For the life of me, I don't know why their friends enjoyed his class," Lana admitted. "The online reviews were pretty mixed, as well. It's just a horrible coincidence. If we hadn't taken his workshop, maybe Chad would still be alive."

"I know you are not supposed to speak ill of the dead, but it's no loss to me. That man was ghastly," Willow said.

Lana silently thanked her lucky stars that her friends didn't know they had briefly dated.

"Let's say Pierre did somehow poison the baguettes. How did he do it?"

Lana asked aloud. "Is it even possible for a poison to act so fast? I mean, Chad didn't go to the bakery with us. He only ate the breads at the picnic and died minutes later. The baker didn't know about The Fussy Gourmet until we got there, so he wouldn't have had time to concoct a poisoned dough ball or tamper with the ingredients beforehand. What do you think, Jane?"

She took a long sip of her merlot, contemplating the situation. "It's easy enough to add something deadly to someone's food, and there are plenty of fast-acting poisons available at any supermarket. Some will kill you in minutes, and others may take a few hours to do permanent damage."

"What do you mean?" Lana asked, incredulous.

"Many household cleaning supplies are fatal in small doses. I noticed several shops that sell those kinds of things close to our hotel. Even a prescription medicine, if administered in high doses, could have caused Chad's delusional behavior, hallucinations, and convulsions."

"But the baker didn't know we were coming," Lana countered.

"Still, he would have rat poison and chemicals for cleaning in his shop. Perhaps Pierre had a heart problem? A massive dosage of digitalis would also have caused Chad's symptoms," Jane mused. "Pierre did leave the workshop space to get the premade loaves from another refrigerator. It would have only taken a few seconds to add something poisonous to the dough, and none of us would have noticed the difference."

"That's a good point, Jane," Willow said, before adding, "Though he would have been taking a great risk that no one else would have eaten from it."

"Yes, but if he was blinded by vengeance, he may have thought this was his one big chance to kill Chad and he didn't want to let it slip by," Lana said, seeing how Pierre could have killed the food critic. "Both Tamara and Miranda did make a big deal about how Chad would taste everything first. Maybe Pierre knew that whatever he added to the dough would be enough to kill Chad almost instantly."

"That's just sick," Willow said, shaking her head.

"To play devil's advocate, any of the other guests could just have easily bought something at a store and added it to the food later," Jane said.

Jane was right, Lana realized. She and Randy had carried all of their baguettes and dips back to the hotel in several plastic sacks. However, during their return taxi ride, she had put the bags in the back of the minivan—in between her guests—while she and Randy squeezed into the narrower front seats. Anyone could have tampered with the food if they were determined to do so.

Lana cast her thoughts back to the first days of the tour and Sabine's need to pet all the animals they came across. "What about something from a hospital's supply room?"

"What do you mean?" Jane asked.

"When I took Sabine to the doctor's office, I caught her coming out of the medical supply room. She said she thought it was the toilet, but she was really nervous about me seeing her."

"Wait—that was the day we went to the Louvre, right? If she was picking up medicines with the intent of killing Chad during the picnic, then she's been planning this for days. That would make it premeditated murder!" Willow exclaimed.

The three women looked at each other, stricken. "Why would someone plan on killing their friend's husband during a romantic week abroad?"

Before they could answer their question, the waiter arrived with their food. Lana wished once again that cameras could record scents because this dish was heavenly. The women's conversations turned to the wonderful food and sights they had enjoyed during their trip so far—and there was plenty of that to discuss. Lana wished she was a better cook so she could re-create some of these dishes at home.

After their meal, Lana ordered a fresh mint tea, while her friends both got a *café au lait*. Her drink arrived with two yellow and orange flowers floating on top of a thick layer of mint leaves.

"What are those?" Lana asked the waiter as he set it down with a flourish.

"Hibiscus and dragon flower blossoms. They don't have much flavor, but are edible and do look quite pretty in the cup," he conceded.

"That's what Miranda made for Chad. Hibiscus tea," Lana mumbled.

"I didn't try that one, but her green tea mint infusion was divine. I'm not entirely certain what she mixed into it, but I swear I tasted cardamom and cinnamon. I'll have to ask her what she added so I can make it at home."

"This one is pretty good, too. They added more mint than I'm used to, but it's nice. Do you want take a sip?" Lana offered.

As her friends sampled her tea, Lana sat back in her chair, her belly full of great food after a pleasant afternoon with two of her best friends. For the first time since this tour started, Lana could feel herself relaxing. She hoped tomorrow would go smoothly. They had a busy day planned, and she wasn't certain where Miranda's head was at. If things got too hairy, Lana figured Sabine would offer to take care of her. Miranda's happiness did seem to be Sabine's number one priority. Lana's thoughts turned to Sabine's husband, Henry. *Poor guy*, Lana thought, *this probably wasn't the Valentine's Day trip he had in mind.*

23

Chartres Cathedral

February 16—Day Five of the Wanderlust Tour in Paris, France

Lana meditated on one of the three rosary windows of Chartres Cathedral, feeling completely at peace. As she took in the exquisite colors and design, Lana wondered how humans could ever make something so impressive, especially without the help of modern tools. Their guide said the cathedral represented the highest architectural and theological aspirations of the Middle Ages in France. Gazing up at the carved stone sculptures, glorious frescoes, and detailed stained-glass windows built into the walls of this awe-inspiring cathedral, Lana believed him. This entire structure was a testament to human determination, imagination, and ingenuity, and it was definitely worth the visit.

The morning had gotten off to a rough start. At breakfast, Miranda had insisted that she wanted to join in the tour, claiming it would help keep her mind off of the paperwork and rigmarole surrounding Chad's death. Lana had worried that this would cause even more problems on their already troublesome tour, and the rest of breakfast hadn't set her mind at ease at all.

During the entire meal, Angie hovered around Miranda, trying to hug her. After Angie attempted to hang a quartz necklace around her neck, Miranda asked her to leave her alone, making it clear that she wasn't interested in crystals or talk of the afterlife. Lana wasn't sure whether it was Miranda's reaction, the shock of watching another human die, guilt over her husband's disputes with Chad, or a combination of all three, but Angie was clearly very shaken.

Once everyone boarded the bus, though, things settled down. The drive quickly took them out of Paris's city center and into the French countryside. Everyone, even Miranda, seemed to be soothed by the one-hour journey through rolling hills, empty fields, and patches of forest. And anytime Miranda teared up, Sabine was there to help her girlfriend get her emotions under control again.

When they stepped off the bus, Miranda locked arms with Tamara and Sabine, then followed their local guide into the church. Angie kept away, giving the new widow space to work through her grief. She and Bernie gravitated towards Lana's friends and spent the tour with them. Once again, Henry hung out with Randy for most of the cathedral tour, talking about baseball, spring training, and their favorite fishing spots.

Once their guided tour ended, the group had time to explore the glorious monument on their own.

Most of Lana's group was scattered around the main cathedral. Only Henry and Randy were climbing the church tower. The views of the Loire Valley, town, and the cathedral's heavy stone buttresses were surely incredible from up there, Lana thought.

Lana kept her focus on the rosary window, absorbing the magnificent "Chartres blue," a color made famous by the cathedral's glaziers. Its deep, rich hue was like none she had ever seen and made the depictions of the biblical stories truly glorious. Their guide had told them 150 of the 176 windows were original, saved from destruction in both world wars thanks to quick-thinking locals who dismantled them piece by piece and brought the glass to safety.

In many of the photos she had seen of the windows, the richly hued glass contrasted wonderfully with the almost black interior, making the windows appear to hover above them. But in 2017, centuries of dirt and grime had been removed and the walls repainted their original eggshell white. Since the completion of that controversial cleaning and renovation, visiting the cathedral was a completely different experience, according to what Lana had read on the flight over. Though the yellowish walls seemed less mysterious and somber, Lana could imagine this was more true to the original builders' wishes to create a light and inviting place of worship.

Just as Lana rose to visit the choir, her phone's alarm told her it was time to return to the bus. She changed direction, in search of her group instead. Angie, Bernie, Willow, and Jane were clustered together at the choir screens in the middle of the transept. She approached her friends, trying to minimize the ticking of her high heels so as not to disturb the many tourists, pilgrims, and locals bowed in prayer.

As she came closer, she heard Angie say, "It is quite different. We really like what we've seen of Seattle so far, but everything is so much closer together, and the weather is far colder. It's going to take us a while to get used to not living on a warm beach. But we wanted to start over and figured Seattle was as far away from Florida as we could get and still be in the continental US."

Jane nodded. "That's true; it is the opposite of sunny Miami. Our beaches are decidedly not warm. I wouldn't want to swim in the Puget Sound without a bodysuit, that's for sure!"

Angie grabbed Bernie's hand. "But it was the best decision we've ever made."

"Why did you move?" Willow asked.

"We were so wrapped up in materialism. Bernie's stress levels were affecting his health, but Western medicines couldn't cure him. If we hadn't found that spa in Arizona, I doubt my Bernie would have gotten through his burnout. The owner is the granddaughter of a real Hopi Indian—can you believe it! And I learned so much from their shaman about quartz therapy, herbal remedies, and meditation. He really inspired me to start my own business."

"It changed our lives for the better," Bernie agreed. "After I sold my restaurants, I felt so lost. Angie and I were even contemplating divorce. Can you believe I almost let this doll go?" Bernie pulled his wife close. "Without taking time away from our daily grind, we never would have reconnected."

So that's what happened, Lana thought. They weren't faking it; they had recently undergone a life-changing transformation. Lana knew from watching co-workers go through a period of burnout how much it could mess with your psyche and sense of self-worth. She was happy to hear Bernie had found a way out of that dark space and discovered a new direction in life.

Willow looked to Jane. "Maybe we should try that. What would you say to a week away?"

"Darling, what do you think this is?" Jane asked.

"Maybe it's the travel time, or simply because everything is so foreign, but this is not the relaxing trip I hoped it would be," Willow conceded. "We haven't had much time to do nothing and just to be together."

"The spa did teach us that it's about making time for each other, no matter where you are or what is going on in your life. And being true to yourself, that might be the most important rule," Bernie enthused.

"That is why we are following our hearts. I'm starting my healing crystals shop, and Bernie is opening his new restaurant," Angie added.

"It sounds like you're pursing your passions. Good for you," Willow said.

"Why, thank you. And it sounds like you've worked quite hard to make your yoga studio a success. Your marketing techniques are quite inspiring. I do hope it all works out for you."

Jane slowly turned to Willow, a shamefaced expression on her face. "She's right. I never stopped to consider how much time and effort you've put into marketing and organizing the classes. You should be proud."

Willow pulled Jane into a hug. "I am, but even more so now that you recognize how hard I'm working to make this happen. Thank you."

Lana's alarm began vibrating again. She went up to the group. "Hey, gang, we are going to have to leave in a minute. Are you ready to go?"

Angie tapped her bag. "I've already shopped 'til I've dropped. Those miniature rosary windows are divine presents."

Willow patted the camera hanging around her neck. "I've taken took many photos on this trip. But I doubt we will be back anytime soon."

"Maybe not Paris, but I do think we need to make an annual vacation a priority, if only to take a week away from work," Jane said. Willow and Lana both looked at her in shock. Then Willow turned to Lana and gave her the biggest grin she'd ever seen. "Thank you," she whispered.

"Thank Dotty," she mouthed back, and Willow nodded.

"Hey Lana, could you take a picture of Jane and me in front of the screens?" Willow asked.

"Sure," Lana said, snapping several photos of her friends. Through the lens, Lana noticed Miranda, Tamara, and Sabine were sitting close to the main altar. Several tourists stood before them, taking selfies of themselves with the *L'Assomption,* a glorious marble statue depicting the assumption of the Virgin Mary to Heaven, adorning the altar, as their background.

"I better let the others know it's time to go. See you at the bus?" Lana asked.

"Sure thing," Angie answered, then turned to Willow. "Could you take a few of Bernie and me, as well?"

Lana moved slowly through the many groups of tourists moving around the aisles, nave, and choir as she approached the popular main altar. When she came closer to the three friends, Lana saw that Miranda was crying. Tamara and Sabine sat on either side of her, hugging their friend tight.

"You are finally free. He hasn't been faithful for years. You deserve better. This is a blessing in disguise, Miranda, it really is. You'll see that soon enough," Tamara said. "It's your time now. Open yourself up to new experiences and live!"

"Tamara's right, this is your chance to find true happiness," Sabine agreed.

"What if I fail?" Miranda asked, shaking her head. "We've been together so long. He's been the scapegoat for all of my problems. And now that he's gone, I'll have no one to blame but myself."

"He had no remorse about leaving you behind," Tamara replied. "It's best for everyone that we ended up in Pierre le Monde's bakery."

Miranda turned to Sabine and cried on her shoulder.

Lana cleared her throat, unsure how to interrupt the three friends. "I'm sorry, ladies, but we need to get back to the bus. Are you ready to go?"

Miranda nodded, doing her best to stop the tears running down her cheeks. Everyone on the tour could tell that Chad was not a good husband, but obviously it was going to take Miranda more time to realize she was better off without him.

"We'll be right there," Sabine said.

"Thanks," Lana said and started to back away.

"Lana?" Miranda said. "This is certainly not the tour I was hoping for, but I appreciate all of your help."

"If there's anything you need, just let me or Randy know," Lana said, eager to get away from Miranda. She had kissed this woman's husband and standing here in this church, Lana was having trouble not confessing to her sins. Now that Chad was dead, Miranda would never find out about their dates unless she told her about them.

As Lana rushed back to the bus, she realized that no one had fought today. That was a tour first, and it left her hoping the last three days of the trip would be smooth sailing, now that Chad was out of the picture.

24

A Liar and a Cheat

Lana was exhausted from the trying week and long day trip to Chartres. Traffic into Paris was backed up due to an accident, meaning their group didn't get back to the hotel until 9 p.m., hours later than planned. She grabbed a sandwich from a café close to the hotel and took it back to her room to eat. When she returned, she noticed Randy and Henry were watching sports in the hotel bar.

Back in her room, Lana kicked her feet up and unwrapped her sandwich. Before she could take her first bite, there was a knock on her door. *What now?* she wondered as she opened it, forgetting to look through the peephole first.

"You were sleeping with my husband! I found your dirty messages on his phone, don't deny it!"

Miranda stood in the hallway, screaming her accusations.

"How could you?" she wailed, staring at Chad's phone in her hand.

Lana grabbed her by the wrist and pulled the emotional woman into her room. Before she could shut her door, several of her guests' heads popped out of theirs. Miranda's words had obviously been heard by many, if not all. *Oh, great*, Lana thought. *Can this terrible tour get any worse?*

"I did not sleep with Chad. I did go out on a few dates with him, but I didn't know he was married," Lana stated as rationally as she could. The last thing she wanted to do was be fired over this stupid mistake. This was certainly the last time she tried online dating.

"I read your flirty messages. Do you really expect me to believe you didn't sleep with him?"

"You'll have to trust me on this, but I assure you, we never had sexual relations of any kind. Heck, we'd only gone out on a few dates. We sent most of those messages to each other when I was in Berlin working another tour."

"Did you request to lead this one, to try to get to Chad?" Miranda asked.

"No! I had no idea he was going to be here. We lied to each other. He didn't know I was a tour guide. And he told me that he worked in computers and was going to be at a conference in Pittsburgh all week. I had no idea he was married or on his way to Paris."

Miranda's chortle sent chills up Lana's spine. "A liar and a cheat. I should have known. I doubt Chad knew what it was to tell the truth."

She sat down heavily on Lana's bed. "His phone's passcode was our anniversary. I didn't think he knew what day it was, but he did." She locked eyes with Lana, wanting to gauge her reaction. "You aren't the only one, you know. He was messaging three other women on the Seattle Singles site."

"I had no idea." Lana blushed, feeling even dirtier than before. How could she have fallen for Chad's charms? The man was a serial womanizer. What was wrong with her?

Miranda's eruption of laughter scared Lana further. "I knew he had messed around on me before, but I had no idea he was capable of juggling four women at once."

"There are no words to express how sorry I am. If I had known he was married, I never would have gone out with him. My ex-husband cheated on me; I know how soul crushing that can be."

Miranda grew quiet as a storm of emotions crossed her face. "Look, I know it's not your fault. It was Chad," she said, staring at his phone, a pensive expression on her face. "I knew he was unhappy. I just didn't think he would go so far as to set up an online dating profile."

Lana couldn't believe how forgiving Miranda was being. If the situation had been reversed, she would probably have tried to rip the other woman's face off. If her guest could be so adult about this, she had no choice but to do the same. "It's too late to send over another guide, but Randy should be able to handle the last few days of the tour. I can imagine my being here will make you uncomfortable."

Miranda whipped her head up. "No, don't go. You shouldn't feel bad about what happened. You didn't know he was married. I understand. You shouldn't lose your job over this."

Lana's jaw dropped. "Are you sure?"

Miranda nodded emphatically. "Positively. You have to stay."

Lana was shocked by the woman's understanding. "Alright. But are your friends going to be okay with me being here?"

"Don't worry. When I show them all of his messages, they will understand that you didn't know what a philanderer he could be."

Lana nodded slowly, trying to get a handle on Miranda's ability to forgive. Another thought made her redden again in shame. If Miranda was going to tell her friends about her and Chad, she would have to tell Willow and Jane about their dates, as well. The last thing she wanted was for one of the guests to slip up and say something. Lana closed her eyes, hoping her friends could be as forgiving as Miranda.

25

Persons of Interest

February 17—Day Six of the Wanderlust Tour in Paris, France

"Inspector, hello." Lana's step faltered. She had just confirmed her group's minivan reservation with the hotel's receptionist when Inspector Boucher entered the lobby and crossed over to her.

"*Bonjour*, Madame Hansen. Do you have a moment to talk?"

"Yes, of course. Have you found out any new information about Chad's death?"

"I have. I would like to speak to your group."

"Sure, they are all in the breakfast hall. We have a tour leaving in forty minutes." Luckily for the inspector, Sabine had just returned from the hospital, where she had gotten her last rabies shot.

"Excellent. That should give us enough time. Take me to them," he said, his tone clipped.

The policeman said something to the waiter, then moments later her group was moved to one large table at the back of the hall, set well away from the hotel's other guests.

He smiled at the group, nodding at Miranda, as he said, "I have news to share with you. We have released Pierre le Monde from police custody."

Miranda gasped. "How could you? He murdered my husband!"

"Our preliminary autopsy results are in. We believe we know what killed

126

your husband, but we were not able to find that substance in le Monde's bakery. Whatever killed Chad must have been added later."

"That can't be! Pierre killed my husband, I am sure of it. I don't know how, but he must have added something to the dough during our workshop."

The detective nodded. "We thought so, too. So I was quite surprised when the lab results showed that none of the baguettes were poisoned. We are still running tests on the rest of the dips and drinks left behind."

The detective pulled out several photographs and spread them out on the table. Next to each dish, plate, and cup was a letter. The officer opened a notebook and said, "I wish to know who made each of the items pictured here."

He started with Tamara, working his way down the row of tourists, writing down all that they had made, drunk, and eaten during the brief picnic. Lana looked at the photographs as she half-listened to the inspector. Something was off, but she couldn't place it. Just as the niggling thought started to turn into a concrete idea, the inspector pointed at her. "What did you make, madame?"

"The baguette with olives and garlic. The third one on the left, marked with a *G*," she explained, pointing at the photograph. "And *L* is my plate. I didn't have anything to drink."

After he finished writing a name down next to each letter, he returned the photos to his briefcase then gazed over his crowd, his expression hard and unforgiving. "I would like to talk to you about who else may have benefited from Chad's death."

"Chad was going to ruin Bernie's restaurant," Sabine said, scowling at the older hippies.

Bernie and Angie were aghast. "That's not true! I'm no amateur. Even if he'd given me a bad write-up, we would have survived it," he said resolutely. "I've run several successful restaurants before and know there are always critics out there that you just can't please. And this new idea is going to be quite profitable, I can feel it."

"Chad said Sabine and Miranda were lovers. I bet she knocked him off so she could have Miranda for herself," Angie said, smirking at Sabine as she spoke.

"That is ridiculous." Sabine grabbed her husband's hand and kissed it. "Henry is my great love. Miranda and I are as close as sisters, and Chad was always jealous of our friendship."

The inspector's pen flew over the page as he wrote down every word.

"Well, Edward left the tour because Chad told him about his wife being a stripper," Bernie said, glaring at Tamara.

The detective looked to the woman, one eyebrow raised. "Why would Chad know this? What is the nature of your relationship with the deceased?"

"We didn't have a relationship! Our families know each other. He found out that I worked at a strip club to pay my way through college. That was it. I didn't sleep with anyone, just danced for them," Tamara said emphatically. Miranda patted her friend's shoulder.

"He did make obnoxious remarks about Jane and Willow's desire to have children," Tamara added.

"He made obnoxious remarks about pretty much everyone on this trip," Jane retorted.

"Lana was seeing my husband," Miranda said, her voice strong.

"He said he was single," Lana rushed to add. "And we only went out a few times. We were never intimate."

Willow and Jane stared at her in disbelief. Lana couldn't look either in the eye. She had been too embarrassed to go to their room and tell them last night. Her plan had been to pull them aside during the day's trip and inform them.

"It must have been a shock to see him and his wife on your tour," the inspector pushed.

Lana snorted. "You could say that," she said, then immediately regretted it. "But not enough of one that I would rather kill him than spend three more days with him."

"Here are the messages they sent to each other," Miranda said, holding out Chad's phone for the inspector.

Lana wanted to disappear; she felt so ashamed. What was going on? Why was she making a big deal about their relationship to the inspector? Last night, Miranda had seemed to understand that she and Chad had not done much more than flirt. She had been so gracious earlier, and now it felt as if she was trying to shove Chad's murder in her shoes.

The inspector chuckled as he scrolled through the many messages Chad and Lana had sent each other. "This is pretty intense flirting for two people who had never met."

Lana reddened even further and cast her eyes to the ground.

"Did you join this tour so you could be close to him?"

"No! If I had known he was going to be here, I never would have agreed to lead it."

"Why didn't you? You must have known the names of your guests."

"I didn't know his last name," Lana replied softly. "We really didn't know each other that well. And he didn't know I was a tour guide, so he wouldn't have been expecting to see me either."

The detective rose and spoke to a fellow officer in French, both watching the guests as they conversed. After a few minutes, he turned back to the group. "If it was not the baker who caused your husband's death, then who else had access to the deceased?" The inspector made eye contact with all of them. "It sounds as if you all had reason to want Monsieur Dumphrey off the tour. Until we know what happened to him, you are all persons of interest."

"You can't be serious!" Henry cried.

The officer glanced across the angry faces staring back at him. "I cannot take you in for questioning without reason, yet I want to ensure you are available if I have further questions. So I am confiscating your passports. We will have the preliminary autopsy reports back this afternoon. I will return once I know more."

"You can't do this!" Bernie growled. His neck was already red, and a vein on his forehead was throbbing. The man had such a temper. Angie stroked his arm, murmuring in his ear to stay calm. Try as he might to come across as an easygoing hippie, his façade was starting to crack, Lana thought. How much longer could he keep up the act?

"Would you rather wait at the police station until the results are known?" the inspector asked Bernie.

Her guest shook his head, but refused to back down. "I am calling our embassy. You don't have the right to keep our passports. We are American citizens, not criminals."

"We will see about that, later this afternoon." The inspector nodded to his fellow officer, who began collecting their passports.

"Are we allowed to continue with our planned tours?" Lana asked.

"I have a copy of your itinerary. If anything changes, you are to call and inform me. I will be in touch."

Angie had to hold her husband back as the inspector exited the breakfast room. He turned on his heel, calling back to Lana's group, "I see you are visiting Musée Rodin this afternoon. Be sure to look at his *Gates to Hell*. His depiction is quite illuminating."

26

Museum Rodin

It took Lana longer than expected to get her group to their first tour of the day. Bernie and Henry both insisted on calling the American embassy to complain about their passports' confiscation, citing their needs to get back to their businesses as the reason for calling. Neither trusted the inspector to return them in time for their flight home. Lana didn't really care why they called; she was just glad they did. The last thing she wanted was to be stuck with this bunch indefinitely.

As soon as the men were ready, she rushed her group onto the bus and set off for the museum. It was a quiet ride over. Lana avoided eye contact with Willow and Jane, still embarrassed about how her friends had found out about her brief relationship with Chad. Sabine sat next to Miranda, obviously trying to distract her by showing her photos of her kennels' adorable occupants. Randy and Henry were discussing the top prospects of the upcoming NFL scouting combine, while Tamara stared blankly out the window.

Dotty had written in her tour notes that the Rodin Museum was one of the most romantic places in the city. When they arrived and walked down the wide cobblestoned path leading to the entrance of the grand mansion before them, Lana had to agree that it was one of the most beautifully situated. It looked more like a small palace than an artist's former home.

By the time they entered the museum and found their guide, their allotted start time had passed. "My next tour starts in forty minutes. I can still squeeze your group in if we get started right away," he said.

"Sure, thank you. I appreciate your flexibility." Lana introduced him to her clients before joining Randy at the back of the group.

"Welcome to Musée Rodin. Auguste Rodin lived and worked in this eighteenth-century mansion, also known as Hotel Biron, for much of his life. His muse and mistress, Camille Claudel, also lived with him here. She was a talented sculptor in her own right, and several of her best works are also displayed in this museum. Please join me now as I show you the highlights of Rodin's work inside, before we tour his gardens where several of his famous works are displayed."

The rooms in Rodin's home were surprisingly cozy considering how large the building was. Most were sparsely decorated, save the many casts, sketches, and smaller statues created by Rodin and Claudel. There was plenty of space left around the exhibited pieces, allowing visitors to circle the sculptures and get quite close to them. Their guide pointed out the sketches Rodin used to create many of his more famous works.

When they reached *The Kiss*, a beautiful statue of two lovers locked in a passionate embrace, their guide explained how it related to Dante's *Divine Comedy* while Sabine pulled her husband aside and kissed him as zealously.

"Lana, could you get a photo of us with this statue? It's as if Rodin captured how Henry makes me feel," Sabine said.

Meanwhile, their guide was stepping into the next room. "Are you coming, Sabine?" Miranda asked as she followed him.

Sabine's smile faltered. Lana could see in her eyes that she was torn.

"They'll be right there, Miranda. It'll just take a moment," Lana said. "Okay, you two lovebirds, smile for me," Lana said, snapping several as they replicated the statue's pose.

Behind her, Lana could hear Miranda clicking her tongue in irritation. *Why can't she let her friend enjoy a little romance?* Lana wondered again. It was as if she didn't want Sabine to be happy.

"I think there are a few keepers," Lana said as she handed the camera back to Sabine. "Okay, folks, we better catch up with the group now," she said, shooing her guests along.

Miranda grabbed onto Sabine's free hand as they walked into the next room. Henry held on as well, making it look like they were playing tug-of-war, with Sabine as the rope.

Their guide showed them a few more highlights inside, before leading them out into Rodin's gardens. Behind the museum was a football field of grass, trees, flower beds, and sculptures. Giant shrubs manicured into fat, circular pyramids were dotted around the space, as were flower beds that Lana imagined would be bursting with color in the spring. Hiding between the bushes were several large statues created by Rodin during his long and illustrious career. Lana couldn't help but mimic *The Thinker*'s pose when she stood under the famous statue of a man sitting with one arm on his knee, his head resting on his fist, frozen in deep concentration. Rodin's ability to convey expression through bronze, stone, and metal was awe-inspiring.

It felt good to be outside in the afternoon sun. There was a slight chill in the air, but the clear skies made it quite pleasant. Which made seeing Rodin's *Gates of Hell* even more disturbing. The metal was so black, it seemed to soak up the sunlight. Writhing naked bodies fighting off devils and monsters as they struggled for their souls filled the double doors. At the top of the doorway was a miniature version of *The Thinker*, casting judgement. According to their guide, Rodin was depicting Dante's horrifying descriptions of Hell and the entrance to Hades. It was so terrifyingly realistic, simply looking at it gave her the shivers.

Lana was standing behind her group, all of whom were taking in the doomed figures, when an unwelcome voice interrupted her viewing pleasure.

"Bonjour, Madame Hansen," Inspector Boucher said.

Lana turned to face him, keeping her expression as neutral as possible. Next to him were two uniformed officers. Lana's stomach sunk; this couldn't be good. "Inspector, it's good to see you again," she lied. "And so soon. Do you have news about Chad?"

"The preliminary autopsy results are in," he said, holding up a file for emphasis.

Miranda took hold of Sabine's hands and bowed her head in prayer.

The inspector looked at Willow's partner. "Jane Jeffries?"

"Yes?"

"We have found a lethal amount of belladonna in his stomach. When our technicians examined the dips and breads from your unfortunate picnic, we found traces of belladonna in only one product—a yogurt and berry dip you made. I need to ask you to come with me," the inspector said.

Willow threw herself in front of her partner. "No way! Jane is a doctor; she took an oath to save lives, not take them!"

"Inspector, you can't be serious," Lana protested.

"This doesn't make any sense," Jane said, shaking her head. "Why would I poison Chad? We just met a few days ago."

The inspector motioned to Tamara and Sabine. "Other members of your tour made clear that he made condescending remarks about your relationship."

"Sure, he made some rude comments, but that's not the first time a stranger has offended me."

He shrugged. "Perhaps you were tired of such remarks and decided enough was enough."

"You can't arrest her!" Willow cried.

"Technically, I can. But she is not under arrest, yet. We wish to speak to your partner first, before deciding whether to press charges."

He looked to Jane. "I wish to understand how this belladonna could have gotten into your dip." He held out his hand as if he was asking her to dance. "Please, would you come with me?"

As Jane nodded, Willow grabbed her arm, restraining her. Jane pried her wife's fingers open. "I am not under arrest. It's better to cooperate so we can get this cleared up as soon as possible. I have nothing to hide. You know I didn't hurt Chad," she said, trying to soothe her partner, who was crying and shaking as the uniformed officers approached Jane from both sides.

"Ms. Jeffries?" the inspector asked, his tone gentle.

"It's Mrs. Jeffries to you," Jane answered, before walking ahead of the officers towards their awaiting car.

"I'll get a lawyer," Willow called out, her voice breaking. Lana wrapped her arms around her friend's shoulders and looked to Randy.

"I can't believe they think Jane killed Chad," Randy said.

"It's got to be a mistake. I'm sure the police will soon realize that Jane had nothing to do with this," Lana said loudly, her tone confident. The last thing they needed was for Miranda and her friends to treat Willow like a pariah.

Lana whispered to her friend, "I need to talk to Randy alone. Are you going to be okay for just a minute?"

Willow nodded, her tears spilling onto the ground. "Jane is my everything. I can't believe this is happening."

"Hey, we're going to do all we can to help her. But first, I need to ask for Randy's assistance. I'll be right back."

"Randy, could you..." Lana nodded her head to the side, and he followed her a few feet away from the rest.

"Man, what are we supposed to do now?" Randy asked.

"The tour must go on. We have to think of the others. Their high tea is booked at the Musée de la Vie Romantique in an hour, and we have Versailles tomorrow. I can't cancel the tour on account of Jane. Dotty would never forgive me."

"In that case, I guess we make the best of it."

"Exactly," Lana said, relieved he understood their predicament. "I think I should call Dotty and see if she can recommend a local lawyer. If they do arrest Jane, I want to be ready. I can imagine Willow will want to go to the police station, especially if they don't release Jane straight away."

"Okay, why don't I accompany the rest of the group to their high tea?"

Lana smiled gratefully, then looked at her watch. "Thank you so much. The minivan will pick you up by the entrance in twenty minutes. The high tea is supposed to take ninety minutes, from start to finish. After you get to the next museum, be sure to let the driver know what time he should return to pick you up."

Randy nodded solemnly. Lana was glad he was taking this task seriously. "Got it."

"I really appreciate you taking care of the group. I'll see you back at the hotel."

27

A Shark in Loose-Fitting Clothes

"Lana, you have to help Jane!" Willow cried. They were back in Lana's hotel room sitting on her bed, their phones and laptops spread around them. Willow had just gotten off the phone with the police, who refused to provide her with any information about Jane's case or condition. The American embassy could only help if Jane was arrested, meaning there was nothing else they could do but wait for the investigator to either let Jane go or charge her formally.

After her increasingly smaller group returned from their high tea, they were officially free for the evening. Randy offered to take over the night shift, in case Jane or Willow needed Lana's help. Lana thanked her lucky stars that Dotty had sent Randy on this tour. The other guides she had worked with were all stellar trip leaders, but they weren't as sensitive or easygoing as Randy was. Considering how badly this tour was going, it was nice to have him here. This week was a true test of everyone's mettle.

"There is no way Jane could have done this," Willow continued.

"Willow, don't worry. I know Jane couldn't harm a soul. She would take them down a notch or two for being rude, but she would never kill them. If the baker didn't do it, then someone on the tour must have. I know it wasn't you, me, or Jane. I'm not so sure about the rest."

Willow nodded gratefully, then took Lana's hands. "Before we talk about who else might have done this, I need to know something. Did you really date that creep? When? And what were you thinking?"

"I met him through that dating app. I wanted to make sure our relationship was going somewhere before I introduced you to him."

"Do you mean Seattle Singles?"

"Yeah, though he wasn't really single, was he? You know me. If I had known he was married, I never would have responded to his messages. This is the last time I try online dating. I'll never be able to trust a man's profile again."

Willow patted her shoulder. "I know you wouldn't have intentionally messed around with a married man. Not after what your ex did to you."

Lana gave her friend a hug, glad that they could move past it so easily. "So if the baker didn't poison Chad, who did? And how did the belladonna get into Jane's dip?" she said. "Someone in our group must have put it in there, but how and when? We were all together during the entire baking workshop."

Willow dabbed at her watery eyes. "Well, I don't think Randy did it," she offered.

"You're right about him. He's new to the job, didn't know any of the guests before we arrived, and has absolutely no motive."

"Let's move on to our horticulture club—Miranda, Tamara, and Sabine," Willow said.

"Tamara was mad at him for ruining her marriage and business."

"What do you mean, her business? I didn't get the impression that she worked."

"I'm not sure what she does, but she told me her husband was about to bail her company out again. Chad ruined that for her, meaning his remarks cost her a husband, home, and livelihood. That sounds like plenty of motive to me," Lana said, as she rose and rummaged around her purse, pulling out a notebook and pen.

"I agree; she was angry with Chad. But is killing him going to get her husband back?"

Lana frowned. "I guess not. But revenge may have made her so desperate and angry that she lashed out."

"Hmm, maybe...." Willow said, clearly not convinced.

"You know what; I'm going to make a list of potential motives. After we're done, I'll see what I can find out about our guests online. Chad's column is published in the *Seattle Chronicle*, and I have a few contacts there I could try asking. Well, maybe I better go through Jeremy; he has good relationships with several of the editors there." When Lana had worked as an investigative reporter for the *Seattle Chronicle*, Jeremy had been her editor. After she was accused of libel, they both lost their jobs.

"Are your old colleagues still convinced you lied about your sources?"

"I'm afraid so. And if they knew I was asking the questions, they may not answer them honestly."

Willow patted her friend's knee. "I'm so sorry."

Lana looked away, fighting back the tears. That had been the most painful part of getting fired—having her co-workers at the newspaper turn their back on her when she needed them most. Several of those who scorned her later in the press were writers and editors she was once glad to call friends.

"At least you and Jeremy are still in touch. I always liked him. Why didn't you two ever date?" Willow asked.

"Because he's married to one of the nicest people you will ever meet and they have three adorable children together."

"Aha. I didn't know he was already hitched."

"To his high school sweetheart, no less." Lana made a show of holding up her notebook. "First on my list: Tamara and Edward. Next up: Sabine. I think she's got a pretty strong motive for wanting to harm Chad. Though maybe she didn't mean to kill him."

Willow looked at Lana, perplexed. "Sabine? The one who's crazy about animals?"

"Yes. She's the one who wanted the Jardin des Plantes tour and asked to switch bakers at the last minute. And I did catch her coming out of the hospital's medical supplies room. Come to think of it, the three of them and our guide really bonded over their visits to Agatha Christie's potent plants garden in Torquay. They all know a lot about poisonous plants. And if they didn't before, our guide explained in detail which ones could kill you and how," Lana said with a frown. "I wish I had paid more attention to what he was saying and what the others were doing while we were in the greenhouse.

We were all together in a room full of plants that could kill; any one of us had the opportunity to steal a few nasty leaves or berries while we were there."

"That would make it more of an opportunity killing than premeditated murder, then, wouldn't it?" Willow mused.

"I guess you're right. Maybe Sabine stole some medicine or plant parts, figuring she might have the opportunity to use it later. Then once she knew Chad would be tasting everything first, she slipped it in the dip."

"But why would she want to kill her best friend's husband?"

"You know, Sabine said something peculiar about how Miranda had to stay with Chad. And she hasn't left Miranda's side since we've been here. Sabine stood by and watched Chad treat her friend horribly, yet she couldn't convince her friend to leave him." Lana looked away. "I think Sabine might be in love with her and decided enough was enough. Miranda had suffered enough humiliation and that it was time to knock off Chad."

Willow looked at her as if she was crazy. "All I see are three good friends who are used to relying on each other. And poisoning someone because they aren't treating your friend right is pretty extreme. She could have encouraged her to get a divorce or at least marriage counseling. Miranda and Chad sure could have used it."

Lana sighed. "Yeah, maybe you're right. It just seems like Sabine prefers Miranda's company to that of her husband."

"I don't know. The way I see it, Miranda keeps having different crises and expects Sabine to drop everything to comfort her. And Sabine treats Miranda like one of the strays she loves to care for. It's too bad she isn't able to put her husband first. He seems like a nice guy, though a bit of a wallflower. What about Miranda? I think we should be investigating her," Willow said.

"I agree with you that Chad was a pretty horrible husband. But Miranda seemed extremely devoted to him. She did say he was dealing with several personal problems right now. Chad's column was recently canceled," Lana explained.

"Okay, I get that he was going through some problems. But Edward made snide comments about Chad's infidelity. It sounds like you aren't the only one he fooled around with. Infidelity is a classic reason for wanting to knock off your spouse," Willow replied.

"Tried to fool around with—nothing happened between us," Lana stated, locking eyes with Willow. "And I don't know. Miranda seemed really torn apart when he died. Besides, if she wanted to kill her husband, why didn't she do it back in Seattle?"

"You could say the same about Sabine or Tamara. Why would either of them wait to kill Chad while they were here on vacation, instead of back home?"

Lana considered the question. "It seems like the men didn't know each other well, which means that they probably didn't tag along when the women were getting together. Yet on this trip, Sabine would have access to him for an entire week. I hate to say it, but I think Sabine poisoned the dip. Or Angie," she added. "I'm still not sure."

"No, not Angie! Why would you suspect her?"

"As soon as that detective showed up, Angie began weeping uncontrollably. Then she and Bernie pointed the finger at everyone else. Perhaps it was guilt, not grief, that was fueling her tears."

Willow began to protest, but Lana talked over her. "Angie is studying herbal medicines, so she would know which ones could kill a man. Bernie's restaurant could have been destroyed if Chad did write a bad review about them. The baker attested to that. And they are investing their life savings in it. They have the most to lose."

"I agree that they have both been affected by Chad's death more than me, but I can't see either one of them murdering anyone. And I still don't believe one review can kill a business. Pierre le Monde's restaurant probably just wasn't very good. He was not the best teacher. And we never did get to taste his baguettes."

"Don't forget about the boat race—it was Bernie who upped the bet," Lana pushed, convincing herself that Bernie might also be desperate enough to harm Chad. As relaxed as Bernie seemed, times of stress certainly revealed that he was a shark underneath his loose-fitting clothes. "And he owned several restaurants in Florida so he must know quite a bit about food preparation. Bernie did taunt Chad into eating his fig baguette creation. Maybe he didn't mean to kill Chad, but only make him sick so he wouldn't be able to join the rest of the tour? That would explain why Angie is so emotional."

"If that's the case, they took an enormous risk, one that didn't quite work out the way they had hoped." Willow looked away, tears in her eyes. "I don't know which one of them wanted to get Chad out of the picture, but I do know my Jane didn't do it. Do you think the police will let me see her?"

Lana wrapped an arm around her friend's shoulder. "I don't know. But you can try. I'm out of my league here. I'm going to call Dotty and see if she can arrange for a lawyer."

Willow squeezed her arm. "Thank you." She rose and pulled on her jacket. "I can't just sit here and wait. I'll call you once I know more, but if you need me, I'll be at the police station."

"I'll let you know what Dotty says once I reach her. In the meantime, I'll see what I can find out about the others. Stay strong, Willow. Jane didn't do this. The police will realize this soon enough."

"I sure hope so. This is not how I expected our romantic week in Paris to go."

"Oh, Willow. It's going to be okay." Lana's heart went out to her friend. She could not imagine how confused and frustrated she was feeling right now.

They embraced once more, then Willow set off to be closer to her partner.

28

Enlisting Help from an Old Friend

Lana's fingers flew over the keyboard. Before she emailed a list of questions to Jeremy, she wanted to check out a few facts.

She had already contacted Dotty, who promised to email Lana a list of lawyers that her own law firm recommended, later this afternoon. Lana hoped that the police would realize they had made a mistake and let Jane go before the day was over. But that French detective seemed quite persistent. Lana was concerned that if he released, he would take another member of the tour in for questioning. And when she looked at the facts, it was entirely possible that she would be the one chosen. He didn't believe that she hadn't asked to lead this tour, in order to be closer to Chad. This trip was already cursed enough; the last thing she needed was to be wrongfully arrested for killing one of her clients.

She quickly worked through her list of questions, starting with Bernie and Angie. She wanted to take a closer look at his businesses. After reading a plethora of articles about his initial successes in Miami and Tampa, she discovered that he had sold some of his restaurants at a loss. *Trendy must not do well long term in Miami, either*, Lana thought. Was that why Chad's critical remarks about his menu and concept had upset him so? Perhaps Bernie knew there was some merit to them.

Next up were Tamara and Edward. The website of her landscape design firm featured some incredible gardens that had been featured in national magazines. Though she had been in business for ten years, her list of projects was exceedingly short. *No wonder Edward had to bail her out again,* Lana thought, *Tamara couldn't find enough clients to make her business profitable.* Yet Chad messed that up for her. Thanks to his remarks, Tamara would lose everything she held dear. She definitely had a motive to harm Chad.

Edward was no prince, either. He was one of several vice presidents of a stock brokerage firm that was currently under investigation by the FCC. *No wonder he was constantly on his phone checking the financial news,* Lana realized, *he was probably worried that he was going to be arrested when he flew home.* Try as she might, Lana could find no information indicating that he would have profited from Chad's death. And though his ego may have been bruised by Chad's revelations about his wife, he would have had no reason to murder Chad for it. He treated her more like a trophy than a partner. Lana wondered whether Tamara even knew about Edward's financial crisis. She doubted it.

Lana had added Henry to her list, simply because he was on the tour. But she couldn't believe the man was capable of hurting a fly. Her online search revealed that he was the owner of a chain of hardware stores dotted around Washington state. According to a feature article in a local small-business owners' magazine, Henry had worked his way up from stock boy to owner, opening his first store when he was in his early thirties. An article in a PAWS publication told of how he met his wife Sabine three years ago while volunteering at one of her animal shelters. Other than his wife, he had no connection to Chad.

It was obvious Henry was not pleased that Sabine rushed to Miranda's aid whenever she looked a touch glum. But would he want to kill Chad because of it? If he thought getting rid of Chad would somehow help get his wife's attention back, he was sorely mistaken. Sabine hadn't left Miranda's side since Chad's soul left his body.

From what Lana could find online, Sabine and Miranda had been friends since high school. Both had attended Washington State University in Pullman and graduated in the same year. Soon after, Miranda had married Chad, a fellow classmate, while Sabine had met and married Henry several years later. Both women lived in Capitol Hill, only a few blocks from each other.

They founded the horticulture club at Volunteer Park, together with Tamara, ten years earlier. From the looks of it, Tamara also lived on the hill, quite close to the park.

Next up was Miranda's family. Lana had written "Bates," Miranda's maiden name, down in her notebook, but not yet looked it up. Her jaw dropped when links about her family filled the screen. Two generations earlier, Grandpa Bates had founded a department store that grew into one of America's favorite places to shop. The chain had stores in every major American city and most small towns. She could imagine that the family was incredibly rich and wasn't surprised to see that they donated millions to charities each year, several of which were run by the Catholic Church. There were even photos of Miranda's father with the pope, taken in Vatican City.

They must be a devout family, she realized. Lana thought back to Chad's jab about Miranda's family and how it was too bad that her dad was still alive. Lana read on, when a sudden thought left her reeling. Divorce was frowned upon by the Catholic Church, as far as she knew. Was that what Sabine meant when she said that Miranda had to let Chad come back? Was Miranda so worried about upsetting her parents or the church that she would rather stay in a bad marriage than seek a divorce?

Lana frowned as she recalled what Tamara had said about Miranda's marriage—that she was staying for the money. Yet Miranda was the rich one, not Chad. Lana puffed out her cheeks and sat still, contemplating the situation.

If the Bates family were able to give millions to charity each year, than Miranda and her five siblings stood to inherit a regal sum. Lana could imagine that the lure of being so wealthy would make anyone stay in line. Especially considering Miranda didn't have another source of income, at least not one she'd talked about during the trip or that Lana could find online. Other than a few parts in plays presented by local theater groups, Miranda seemed to spend most of her time on her horticulture club.

Lana thought back to all of Chad's humiliating brushoffs and condescending remarks that Miranda had put up with during the tour. They were not good together. Lana could see Miranda not wanting to upset her parents by getting a divorce, if that was against their religious beliefs. But murder was an even more frowned-upon sin. Besides, divorce wasn't their only option; they could have lived apart instead.

What about Chad's restaurant? Was that a lie told to pester Bernie and Miranda? Lana wouldn't be shocked if it was. She found no further mention of his supposed restaurant, nor any news of a new business deal. However, Lana knew that didn't mean much. If whatever deal he was negotiating had fallen through, it probably wouldn't have been featured in the news. Lana did find hundreds of reviews written by The Fussy Gourmet and published in the *Seattle Chronicle*. The most recent was dated four days ago. Lana stared in bewilderment at the screen. Miranda had said his column was recently canceled, yet here was a degrading review of a café that had opened on the Seattle Waterfront a week earlier. This couldn't be an older piece; Chad must have prepared this review for publication just before he left for Paris.

That's odd, Lana thought. Miranda had said he was quite upset about both a business deal falling through and his column being canceled. Could she have simply said it wrong? Heck, perhaps Chad had lied about that, too, in order to garner Miranda's sympathy. Though if the *Seattle Chronicle* was considering canceling his column, Lana could imagine that even the possibility would upset Chad. Yet when she thought back on his behavior these past few days, he hadn't seemed distraught—more like exceedingly self-confident.

At last, Lana typed in "belladonna." Their guide at the Jardin des Plantes had talked about its poisonous properties in detail during their tour, but he had shared far too much information for her to remember it all. If that was the plant that killed Chad, she should know more about its effects on the human body, she reckoned.

When images of the plant appeared on screen, Lana recalled it immediately. It was the bush with gorgeous purple flowers and black berries. According to the information she found online, every part of the plant was deadly. Yet it was also used to treat cancer and asthma patients, as well as alleviate motion sickness. That was why Jane had those belladonna drops, to help her with the plane and boat rides. Lana frowned a little when she read its use as a homeopathic remedy was discouraged because the dosing was uncertain and had often been recalled due to unsafe levels.

Lana pursed her lips. If the police were to search Jane's room and find the drops in her luggage, she could end up in custody longer than expected. After she was finished with this email, she would have to ask at reception whether it was possible to be let into Jane and Willow's room. Perhaps she could remove any herbal medicines from their suitcases before the police thought to examine their contents. Lana was certain her friend hadn't harmed Chad, but she was not convinced that the police would believe Jane had nothing to do with his death.

Unable to find out more about Chad's column, restaurant, or deal, Lana opened up her email and typed in a few questions for her friend Jeremy. Since they had gotten back in touch a few months earlier, they had lunched together twice, and Lana had even babysat his adorable children once. He was still friendly with several of their old colleagues at the *Seattle Chronicle*. If anyone could find out about Chad's column and deal, it would be Jeremy.

29

The Inspector Returns

After Lana sent off her email to Jeremy, she pulled out the thick brochure about Versailles that Dotty had given her and slowly flipped through the colorful photos. It looked incredible, but gigantic. Tomorrow was going to be a long day. If everyone got along, the day would be infinitely better. Before she could get past page fifteen, her phone rang. Lana shuddered instinctively, wondering what crisis was in store for her next.

"Yes, this is Lana," she said, expecting to hear one of her guests on the line. Randy would have simply knocked.

"This is Inspector Boucher. I am in your lobby. Could you come down to meet me?"

"Sure, be right there." Lana hung up and rushed downstairs, hoping he had Jane and Willow with him.

Unfortunately, he was alone.

"What can I do for you, Inspector?"

He handed Lana a pile of passports. "Two of your guests contacted your embassy and complained about my confiscation of your passports. I may not have the right to keep these, but I have relayed your information to French customs authorities. None of you may leave Paris before your scheduled flight."

"We are leaving in two days," Lana stated.

"Our lab knows. We cannot stop you, but do expect to know exactly what caused Chad's heart failure within twenty-four hours."

"Wait, I thought it was the belladonna."

The inspector sucked in his breath and looked away, as if he was not entirely certain he wanted to continue this conversation.

"That's what you said when you took Jane in," Lana pushed. "If it's not the belladonna, why haven't you released her?"

"We found traces of another toxic substance, but the quantities were too low to have caused Chad's death. Our technicians still believe the belladonna was the culprit. However, we are retesting several samples before drawing our conclusions," he admitted, adding quickly, "We will continue to hold your friend in our custody until we know for certain what caused Chad's death."

"What about her partner, Willow? Is she allowed to see Jane?"

"Willow Jeffries refuses to leave our waiting room even though we will not grant her access to her partner at this time. It is her choice; we won't rush our decision on account of her."

"I don't understand why you are detaining Jane. She had absolutely no reason to harm Chad."

"Perhaps, but she is the only one with belladonna in her luggage, along with several other herbal remedies that are fatal in high doses. She was obviously familiar with their use."

Drat, Lana thought, *so much for destroying anything that could reflect badly on Jane.* "She's a doctor, of course she is! Besides, Jane isn't the only one on the trip with knowledge about poisonous plants. Heck, three of the women on my tour grow deadly plants in their gardens, and Angie is studying herbal medicine. Any one of them would have known that belladonna is lethal. And if they didn't before, our guide at the botanical gardens explained in detail which plants in their collection were killers. Based on your logic, any of us had access and thus could have done it!"

The inspector's eyes narrowed. "You make a good point. What exactly was your relationship with the deceased?"

Lana sucked in her breath. This was not the way she had expected the conversation to go. "I told you before, we started chatting through a dating website several weeks ago, but we didn't meet until I returned from another trip, about three weeks before I set out for Paris."

"How could you not know that your new lover was on your upcoming trip, along with his wife?"

"First, he was not my lover. We only went out a few times. And second, the website we met through is called Seattle Singles. I had no reason to believe that he was married, nor did I know his last name. There are a lot of Chads in the world."

"Still, it is a most unusual coincidence. I do not believe –"

"Inspector, thank goodness! We were just trying to find Lana so we could get in touch with you," Angie panted, as she rushed towards them. "You have to let poor Jane go. She did not harm Chad!"

"Madame, how can you be so certain?"

Angie looked to the floor as her tears hit the carpet. When she responded, Lana was not entirely certain that she heard Angie correctly. "Because I am responsible for his death."

Lana's eyes widened in shock. She was right; Angie had killed him because of his threats to destroy Bernie's new business! As glad as she was to see Jane go free, she couldn't help but feel bad that Angie had felt compelled to murder someone in order to save her husband. Lana placed her arm on the older woman's shoulder just as her husband burst into the lobby.

"Whatever my wife is confessing to, she doesn't mean it!" Bernie yelled as he jogged over to Angie.

"Yes, I do, Bernie," she insisted. "It was my stupid idea. I read about it online and convinced Bernie to help me make it. But I couldn't live with myself if Jane paid for our crime."

"Madame, what are you talking about? Did you make a poison? Where is this murder weapon?"

As Angie opened her purse, the officer grabbed her hand and took the bag from her. He looked inside before removing a small doll dressed in men's clothing. A piece of human hair was tied around its neck, and a pin stuck out of its chest.

"He died of a heart attack, didn't he?" Angie wept. "I took a piece of hair from Chad's jacket after he insulted Bernie in the market. I'd read about these voodoo dolls online, but we didn't realize how powerful they could be. I just wanted to curse him, not kill him."

Lana looked to the police officer, who was staring at Angie as if she was bonkers. He shook his head and slowly handed the doll back to Angie.

She recoiled, unwilling to touch it. "It's cursed! We have to burn it to destroy its potency."

The officer gazed at her quizzically. "Madame, why did you make this doll? Has Chad wronged you?"

"He was evil," Angie hissed. "He threatened to write a bad review about my husband's restaurant. It hasn't even opened yet! He would have destroyed us. One bad review from Chad will do that to you."

"So if you kill him now, he cannot write this bad review, *non?*"

"Yes. I mean, no! We didn't mean to kill him!" Angie said, her eyes fixated on the voodoo doll.

"Interesting," the detective said. "I will take this in as evidence, but I am not going to take you in for questioning at this time." He glanced at the doll again, before adding, "Your tour is traveling to Versailles tomorrow?"

"Yes," Lana confirmed. "We are leaving early in the morning."

"Enjoy your journey. I will visit with you again after you return." He bid them *adieu*, whistling the French national anthem as he walked out of the hotel.

30

Afternoon Tea at Versailles

February 18—Day Seven of the Wanderlust Tour in Versailles, France

Lana gazed out at the French countryside, unseeing. Their bus ride to Versailles was pleasant enough, but she was having difficulty enjoying the beauty outside her window. Her mind kept turning over the facts she had learned about her guests, and who would have had enough of a motive to harm Chad.

Last night, after the inspector left, Lana had looked into Pierre le Monde's patisserie and work history. She was not convinced that The Fussy Gourmet's review destroyed him, as he claimed. Yet, after looking at the evidence, she understood why Pierre was so angry with Chad. Three days after Chad's degrading review of le Monde's patisserie was published in the *Seattle Chronicle*, a small article in the financial section announced that the investors poised to fund his chain pulled out of their agreement and invested in one of his competitors instead—a local baker who received a glowing review from Chad.

Geez, Lana thought, *I had no idea a reviewer had so much power.* Although Lana sincerely doubted that anything supernatural had caused Chad's death, she no longer thought Angie had been off the mark when she made that voodoo doll. Luckily, the bus ride gave her plenty of time to think on the case. It helped that her guests were pretty quiet this morning, even though their silence was due to more than just their early departure time.

After breakfast, Lana had ushered her group outside to the awaiting bus. She got on first, standing behind the driver to allow her guests to enter while she conferred with him about the travel time and traffic conditions. Angie and Bernie headed to the back and stretched out. Randy took a seat in the middle, and the three girlfriends sat together in the front, with Miranda and Sabine sitting next to each other and Tamara just behind them. Henry climbed in last.

Randy patted the chair next to him. "I've got room here," he said jovially.

"I was hoping to sit with my wife," Henry responded, staring at Miranda.

Sabine looked up at Henry's words, just as Miranda grabbed her hand and held on tight. Lana's forehead creased. Was Miranda truly so reliant on Sabine, or was she taking advantage of the situation? It was difficult to tell.

"Oh, Miranda needs me right now. I thought you understood."

"She always needs you. Tamara can hold her hand for a few hours. This is supposed to be a romantic trip abroad, and so far I've spent more time with Randy than you. We only have two more days in Paris. I want to spend time with my wife before we fly home," Henry said, his tone firm. Lana was shocked. This was the first time he had put his foot down about anything since the tour began.

Sabine must have been surprised, too, because she stood up immediately, wrestled her hand loose from Miranda's grip, and went to her husband. "Oh, pooh bear. I have been ignoring you, haven't I? You're right. We do need some 'we time,'" she cooed, grabbing his arm and pulling him towards the back.

Randy moved up closer to the front in order to give them some space. Tamara sat next to Miranda, who was staring straight ahead, her arms crossed over her chest and her bottom lip sticking out. Lana was disgusted by her childish behavior. *Why can't she let Sabine and Henry enjoy their trip together?* she wondered.

After everyone was seated and the driver was ready to leave, Lana walked over to her fellow guide, smiling. "Can I be your seatmate?"

"That would be great." Randy shoved his backpack under his seat to make room for her, then leaned in close to her ear. "Boy, I'm sure glad to see Henry being more assertive. Miranda has been leaning on Sabine the whole trip. And worse, from what Henry told me, she's always coming over to their house and calls Sabine several times a day. He rarely gets to be alone with his own wife."

"Wow, that's pretty intense. I bet it's hard on their marriage, too. Sabine is so quick to abandon Henry to take care of Miranda."

Lana looked to Miranda, sitting three rows ahead of them. She and Tamara had their heads close together and were whispering conspiratorially. Behind them, Henry and Sabine were cuddling happily while chatting about the scenery going by.

"It is quite manipulative behavior, in my opinion," Randy whispered. "If I were Henry, I would ask to have more Miranda-free days."

Lana nodded in agreement. At the beginning of the tour, Miranda had seemed to be the innocent, emotionally traumatized victim of a distant and cold husband. Perhaps Miranda was not as fragile and weak as she appeared to be.

She was, however, continually doing things to elicit sympathy from Sabine. Up until now, Lana had thought Sabine was Miranda's protector. But perhaps she was merely her security blanket. Would Sabine really harm Chad, especially of her own volition? The more she thought about it, the more she doubted that the thought of killing Chad to free Miranda from his wrath would have even crossed Sabine's mind. Yet she was the one who had requested both the horticulture tour and baking workshop. At least, she was the one who had contacted Wanderlust Tours about them. But who was the real instigator behind those additions—Sabine or Miranda? Lana vowed to find out today. Jane's freedom may depend on knowing the answer.

Before she could ask Randy what he thought about Sabine and Miranda's relationship, Angie called out from the back, "Lana, how long is the trip, anyway? And is there a working bathroom on the bus?"

"Shoot," Lana mumbled, scolding herself. She'd gotten so caught up in her thoughts she'd forgotten to introduce their next destination to her guests. She made her way to the front of the long bus and turned on the microphone.

There weren't many guests left, but there was so much road noise, it was easier to use the announcement system than yell.

"Ladies and gentlemen, we are about twenty minutes away from Versailles. We have a guided tour of the main palace, royal gardens, and the Queen's Hamlet, which was Marie Antoinette's private residence. The grounds are quite extensive, and the buildings are spread apart, meaning we will be doing a lot of walking. But we'll have plenty of time for snack breaks."

Angie tentatively raised her hand.

"And there are many toilets dotted throughout the complex, as well as here on this bus. It's in the middle, at the bottom of the staircase," Lana added, pointing towards the "WC" sign. Angie smiled in appreciation and lowered her arm.

"Our guide will be able to tell you more about the turbulent history of Versailles, its role in the French Revolution, and the many kings and queens who once lived there. I do have a few brochures, if anyone is interested in reading up on it before we arrive," Lana finished, waiting to see who would want to bone up. Angie and Tamara raised their hands. Sabine and Henry were so focused on each other, Lana doubted they had heard her brief speech.

Lana gave a brochure to each guest, then took her place next to Randy for the last few minutes of their journey. As their bus approached the main gates, Lana could feel her jaw dropping as her eyes took in the magnitude of the palace before her. Was this colossal, decadent structure really built to house just the French monarch and his family? *An entire village could fit inside*, she thought.

After her group was dropped off close to the main gates, it took Lana several minutes to find their local guide standing among the many hovering before the entrance. Once she did, he got them through security and inside the palace in record time. As soon as they'd regrouped, he began his upbeat tour by sharing more about the history of Versailles.

Lana listened in fascination as he explained how Versailles was the primary residence of the kings of France for one hundred years, until the French Revolution. The hunting lodge originally built on this site was transformed into a chateau by Louis XIII, who also expanded the gardens. King Louis

XIV, also known as the Sun King, expanded it into the palace we know today. It took twenty years to expand and renovate the palace and forty to complete the magnificent gardens.

As their guide led them through the many rooms the public was allowed access to, Lana was amazed to see that every inch of the walls, ceilings, and floors was covered in tapestries, decorations, or paint. Vibrant frescoes covered most of the ceilings. And the rest was filled in with gold. The precious metal was clearly the Sun King's favorite; Lana had never seen so much gold leaf in her life. She wasn't surprised to see the private rooms were as lavish as the public chambers.

All of it was amazing, but Lana's favorite was the Hall of Mirrors. That alone was worth the visit. It was a room at the back of the palace, facing the gardens. One wall of the long and rather narrow space was covered with enormous mirrors. Several crystal chandeliers hung between richly painted frescoes. Everything sparkled and shimmered. Lana had never seen such an incredible dance of light. Their guide said it was a tribute to the Sun King and designed to reflect sunlight back into the gardens. Lana knew that if she lived there, she would spend a lot of time in that room.

Throughout the tour, Henry and Sabine walked arm in arm, with Miranda and Tamara trailing far behind them. All four seemed to be enjoying the tour, though they didn't say much. Angie and Bernie, on the other hand, were so enthusiastic about everything they were seeing, they couldn't stop asking questions about the history of the palace and residents. Lana was thrilled to see her guests were enjoying themselves so thoroughly but did wonder whether they would have time to see the gardens and Marie Antoinette's residence, as well. There was so much to see and learn, the palace alone was worth spending a full day.

As they were finishing up their tour of the main palace, their guide announced, "We are now going to visit the royal gardens, considered by many to be the jewel of Versailles. Most of the flowers are not yet in bloom, but it is still magnificent. And in this time of the year, the landscape design is even clearer. These gardens are one of the finest examples of the classic French garden style remaining today. There are also many important statues and fountains spread throughout. At the back are the private gardens and residence of Marie Antoinette, the last queen of France. She was also beheaded during the French Revolution, nine months after her husband, King Louis XVI."

"Let them eat cake," Miranda muttered to Tamara and laughed.

When their guide took them outside, Lana's eyes about popped out of her head. The gardens stretched on forever. *They must be several football fields long and wide,* she thought. And every square foot was covered in trees, plants, and shrubs, all meticulously manicured into fanciful shapes and patterns. It was magnificent.

Her guide led them over to an incredible display of stone horses dancing in a frothy fountain. Statues of Greek-looking ladies dressed in flowing robes stood on pedestals, admiring themselves in stone mirrors. An edge of gold ran along the palace's rooftop, shimmering in the morning sun.

Their guide had just launched into his next speech about the fountains and sculptures, when Lana's phone rang. She looked to see who was calling and was excited to find that it was Jeremy getting back to her. She answered, quickly saying, "Hi, Jeremy, give me just a second," before rushing over to her fellow tour guide. "Hey, Randy, I need to take this phone call. I'll catch up in a minute. Is that okay?"

"Of course, Lana," he said, smiling easily. She was glad he was relaxing into his role. As their guide began moving again, she followed along behind her group, not wanting her conversation to interrupt his explanation about the garden's history and layout.

"Hello, Lana. It's good to hear from you," Jeremy said.

Lana covered one ear to hear him better. Despite the size of the gardens, it was quite busy, and there was a lot of noise from tourists, guides, and children.

"Boy, you sure know what questions to ask. It took two vodkas to get it out of Frankie, but she finally let slip that our old editor-in-chief is livid. Chad is going to write a new column for *The New Yorker*. They want him to review restaurants across America, not just in Seattle. There goes their local celebrity critic. *The New Yorker* even agreed to help finance his dream restaurant in Manhattan, and there's talk of him hosting a television show, as well."

"Wait, his business deal *did* go through?" Lana said, her voice rising in surprise. Miranda and Tamara, the closest to her, looked back to see what she was getting worked up about.

Lana smiled and covered the phone. "Everything's fine. I'll be right back," she said, then moved farther away from her group. The last thing she wanted was for Miranda to find out that she was investigating her husband.

"Yes. It's still hush-hush, but the *Seattle Chronicle* is reeling. I guess they didn't know Chad had begun negotiations with *The New Yorker*. Frankie said they only found out after Chad asked to have his mail forwarded to a New York address, and bragged to the human resources department about how the magazine paid for the apartment."

"Oh, my. So he was really moving to New York, and apparently soon if he was already having his mail forwarded there."

"It sure sounds like it," Jeremy agreed.

"You didn't tell her that Chad is dead, right?" she asked.

"No way. I don't want to get involved with that mess. I did mention that she should check the foreign wire, in particular any French obituaries mentioning American citizens."

"Hmmm." Frankie was one of those Lana had considered to be a close friend, until she was fired from the newspaper. Since then, Frankie wouldn't return her calls.

"Come on, she deserves a little quid pro quo. She's going to find out about it eventually. At least this way, they'll have the scoop. It would be embarrassing if the *Seattle Chronicle* didn't know. They've been running his columns for almost twenty years now."

"That's true. I would offer to give her a firsthand account of his death, but the last time we spoke, Frankie called me a disgrace to journalists everywhere."

"One day, Lana, the truth will come out, and the world will know that you did not lie about your sources. But for now, I have to go to work."

"Wait, did you find anything else out about the Bates family and divorce?"

"Oh, yeah, that was a strange question. I asked my society editor about it. It took her some digging, but she found an old article about Miranda's oldest sister in the morgue," Jeremy said, referring to a newspaper's historical archives.

"Twenty years earlier, the woman had been disowned by her family after divorcing her husband. She wrote an exposé about her family, but the Bateses were apparently able to suppress it because the book is no longer for sale at any major retailers. Apparently she was quite a party girl. My editor found another article recounting the sister's extreme lifestyle of alcohol and drug abuse. She was no good Catholic, that is for certain," Jeremy quipped.

"Maybe her divorcing her husband wasn't the only reason she was disowned," Lana mused aloud.

"I tend to agree with you," Jeremy said. "But I have to hit the road, kid. Take care of yourself, you hear?"

"Will do. And when I'm back in Seattle, the coffee is on me."

"I'll take you up on that. Enjoy Paris!"

Lana hung up, gazing unseeingly at the flower beds, and thought over what Jeremy had just told her and everything she had seen on this trip.

She recalled Chad's remarks at the market about how there were many things he had not shared with his wife – and the doozy of an argument they'd had later that night. What if the fight had been because Chad let it slip that his new restaurant was in New York? It hadn't sounded like Miranda was part of his plans for his new life. If she had found out about his fresh start, would she have accepted his need to move on with grace? Would she have tried to worm her way into his new life? Or would his lies and rejection, after her years of devotion, have pushed her over the edge?

Murder just seemed so extreme, though. Why not simply live separately, if a divorce would put Miranda's life as a rich socialite in jeopardy like it had done to her sister? And after all, Chad had been juggling four girlfriends. He almost certainly wouldn't have wanted a divorce in order to marry someone else.

Yet, if Miranda's parents were to find out about their separation, they might still threaten to disown her. Millions of dollars were potentially on the line. And Miranda had put up with his horrid behavior throughout the trip, only to learn he was making plans without her. *Hell hath no fury like a woman scorned*, Lana mused.

She was so lost in these morbid thoughts that she didn't see or hear Miranda approaching until she spoke. "Who was that on the phone?" her guest asked.

Lana's heart jumped. "Oh, an old co-worker," she said, blushing. *How long had Miranda been standing there?* she wondered, embarrassed to realize that she possibly knew more about Chad's future plans than his wife did.

Miranda's eyes narrowed as she waited for Lana to continue. When she didn't, her guest broke into a smile. "What do you think of the gardens?"

"They are absolutely gorgeous. I couldn't even guess how many gardeners they need to keep this place in shape."

Miranda gazed at the manicured trees, shrubs, and plants filling the expansive grounds. "Wouldn't that be the most amazing job?" she said dreamily.

"It sure would," Lana replied, fibbing to keep her client happy. She had a black thumb, not a green one. After coming home to a houseful of dead plants last month, she'd gotten rid of all of them, figuring she'd be better off planting bulbs and flowering shrubs outside of her windows and letting nature take care of the rest.

"Hey, Tamara, did you see how they trimmed those bushes? They almost look like apostrophes," Miranda said as she darted back to her friend. Lana also caught up with the group, albeit more slowly as she contemplated all she had learned. Jane was no killer, but who was? As much as she wanted to point the finger at another guest in order to see her friend set free, she couldn't do so unless she was entirely certain of who had done it and how.

As much as Lana wanted to believe Sabine had poisoned Chad in order to protect her friend—or that Angie had done it to protect her husband—she was having second thoughts. Miranda had a far stronger motive for wanting to get rid of Chad than Lana had originally thought. If he was demanding a divorce, then murdering him would be the only way of ensuring she inherited her share of the family fortune.

Their guide led them along the white paths snaking through the gardens, pointing out a statue or plant as they went. Soon all of them were dragging their feet. When Lana looked back towards the palace, they were so far away that she could finally appreciate how massive the building and gardens were. The Sun King's contribution to classic French architecture and landscape architecture would never be forgotten.

Lana was just about to ask whether there was a café nearby, when their guide stopped and turned to his group. "Before we continue our tour of Marie Antoinette's private gardens and residence, would you like to take a break?"

"Yes, I could use a coffee and a toilet," Bernie said.

"There's a café and facilities just around the corner. Why don't we take a half-hour rest, then continue on?"

"Excellent idea, thank you," Lana said, speaking for the group. She sure could use a minute to sit and put her feet up, and by the looks of it, so could all of her guests.

Their guide led Lana's group to a small food stand with a takeaway window and outdoor seating. After pointing Bernie and Angie to the toilet, their guide pulled Lana and Randy aside. "If you do not mind, I have to call my boss. There has been a change with my next group's itinerary, and he needs to speak to me about it. Is this is a good time? I'll be back within twenty minutes."

"Certainly, take your time. We'll wait for you here," Lana said with a smile, understanding completely. When he stepped away to make his call, she turned to Randy. "It looks like it's takeaway. Why don't we set up a table for our guests, then get their orders?"

"Sounds good. I'll get the tables sorted. Hopefully they have some in the sun. It feels great right now."

"Excellent," Lana said, as she returned to their group, clustered together close to the takeaway window. Tamara was showing something to Miranda on her phone. Whatever it was had both women laughing. Henry was holding his wife's hand, watching tiny birds dart between the tables. Sabine was looking around, searching for something. "Can I help you?" Lana asked.

"I don't see a toilet sign. Do you know where it's at?"

"Yes, it is kind of hidden," Lana said as she walked around to the back of the café. A small "WC" sign hung on one door. She held the door open for her guest, then realized what a golden opportunity this was. Miranda had been glued to her side for so much of the trip, this was the first chance she'd had to talk to Sabine alone since Chad's death.

Earlier, she had thought perhaps Sabine had killed Chad in order to protect her friend. After all, Sabine had requested that they change bakers and had acted so nervous at the hospital. But now that Lana knew about Chad's intentions and Miranda's background, she was having second thoughts. Maybe Miranda had sweet-talked her best friend into helping her get rid of Chad, either planning it before the trip even began or coming up with the idea after his horrible behavior on the tour.

Curiosity about Sabine's role in this mess drove her into the bathroom.

As soon as Sabine exited a stall, Lana touched up her makeup in the mirror. As casually as she could, she said, "I just have to know—what did you think of Pierre le Monde?"

"That's an odd question," Sabine replied while washing her hands. "Why do you ask?"

"I'm a little surprised your friends recommended his workshop. He is quite intense."

"If you must know, Miranda's tennis instructor was raving about Pierre," Sabine said, keeping her gaze fixed on her hair. "He must have had a better experience."

"But you asked me to change the reservation, not Miranda."

Sabine shrugged. "Miranda and Chad had just had a horrible fight, and she was upset. I wanted to take care of it for her."

"What were they fighting about?"

Sabine chuckled. "What didn't they fight about? I don't know what set off that particular argument, but it was a nasty one."

"You two are so close. Was Chad ever jealous?"

Sabine laughed bitterly. "Constantly. He never understood us. He was convinced we were more than roommates in college. Can you believe it?"

"But you weren't?"

161

"No! Miranda helped me get out of an abusive relationship my first year of college. It took years of therapy before I could trust men again. Miranda was always there for me. And then I met Henry." Sabine smiled wistfully. "When things started going wrong between her and Chad, I returned the favor. If Chad had been kinder to her, Miranda wouldn't have sought solace from me so often."

Poor Henry, Lana thought, wondering whether he'd known what he was getting into when he'd married Sabine. "You really are a good friend to her." Lana nodded encouragingly, afraid her guest might close up again. "Sabine, I need to ask: Why did you go into the medical supply room at the hospital? What were you looking for?" Lana hoped she wasn't pushing her luck.

Sabine seemed shocked and began shaking her head.

"Please don't deny it. I saw you coming out of the supply room. If you don't tell me what you were looking for, I'll have to tell the inspector. I don't believe Jane poisoned Chad, but someone on this tour did."

"It wasn't me!" Sabine exclaimed, then blushed and looked away. "I wanted to steal some sleeping pills. I forgot mine at home, and the jet lag is making sleep difficult. But I don't know the word for them in French, so it was a wasted effort." She shrugged in embarrassment.

"Which one of you requested the poisonous plants tour?" Lana asked, hoping to get more information out of her before Miranda noticed they were gone.

"We all wanted to see it," Sabine said, but her voice trembled.

"But who said you should call Wanderlust Tours?"

Sabine's brow knitted together as she remembered. "Miranda," she whispered, then quickly put her hand over her mouth. But it was too late. Lana heard her answer. Her face drained of color as the truth sunk in. Sabine wasn't behind the plant tour or the change in the baking workshop, Miranda was.

Both women jumped as the door opened and Miranda walked into the bathroom. "Oh, there you two are," she said.

"We're just finishing up. I better get back to the group," Lana said as casually as she could, hoping her voice didn't betray her nervousness. Miranda must have poisoned her husband or, at the very least, must have had a hand in his demise. But had she meant to kill him? And how had she administered the belladonna or whatever else may have made him so sick?

"Randy's set up a table for us, towards the back of the terrace," Miranda said.

"Great, thanks," Lana responded, then scampered out of the bathroom.

31

Do Fish Sunbathe?

Lana was so confused. Here she had thought Sabine was the quiet mastermind behind Chad's demise, when in reality, Miranda had most likely poisoned her husband and somehow managed to frame Jane for it. *But how?* Lana's mind was reeling with questions and possibilities.

Why had Miranda insisted they take a baking workshop with Pierre le Monde? Was it a lucky coincidence, or had she known how The Fussy Gourmet ruined his patisserie? In the few reviews Lana had read, the man was extremely critical, and few restaurants escaped his wrath. His annual list of the top ten restaurants in Seattle had only included eight last year because he hadn't thought any of the others he had reviewed were worthy.

But how many of those Chad criticized in his column actually went belly up? Lana could imagine there were only a handful. If Chad had kept a list, Miranda may have known about it and even had access to it. And the Chad she'd met on this trip was definitely the kind of person who would keep track of those he had ruined, as a point of pride.

But if Miranda did intentionally choose le Monde because Chad ruined him, then she must have done so in the hopes of setting up the baker to take the fall for Chad's death. *That would make it premeditated murder,* Lana realized.

She slowed her pace, wanting to think this through before she rejoined her group. If Miranda had poisoned Chad, how had she done it? It couldn't have been the tea. She'd offered it to Bernie, as well. Or had she figured that if the Floridian drank it, too, his death would be a diversion?

The police had only found traces of belladonna in Jane's dip. They'd mentioned finding traces of another poison, but had yet to share with Lana what it was or in which product they'd found it.

If it was Jane's dip that had killed him, how had Miranda gotten belladonna into it? During the workshop, they had been all working side by side and using the same bowls of ingredients, all placed in the center of the stainless steel countertop. Heck, they kept bumping elbows, they were working so close together. Someone would have noticed if Miranda had added ingredients to Jane's dip.

Besides, they had also been sampling their own dips and tapenades as they worked, adding more ingredients as necessary, until they were satisfied. If Miranda had put belladonna into the dip during the workshop, chances were great that Jane would have died before the picnic even began.

When Lana saw Miranda and Sabine exiting the bathroom, deep in conversation, she hurried back to the terrace. Though most of the tables were occupied, Randy managed to find three in the warm sun.

"This is great, thank you," Lana said.

"No problem. I'm glad we are taking a short break before touring Marie Antoinette's gardens. They look even prettier than the ones we just walked through, but also quite large," he said.

Sabine and Miranda soon returned, but avoided Lana. She hoped her brief interrogation of Sabine wouldn't get her into trouble later.

Lana glanced at the menu and saw they offered a small selection of teas, cakes, and coffees.

"What a lovely selection," Lana said loudly, capturing her group's attention. "If you know what you want, I'll order everything at once." Lana pulled out her notebook and flipped past her to-do list, using the next blank page to record her guests' orders.

"The hibiscus tea and cake combination sounds nice," Tamara said.

Sabine nodded in agreement.

Miranda said, "Make that three. Lana, you should try it. A splash of honey tempers the bitterness of the hibiscus. It's quite refreshing."

"Sounds good. Thanks for the suggestion, Miranda," Lana said, trying to act as normal as possible. Until she figured out how Miranda could have poisoned Chad, there was no point in alerting the woman to her suspicions.

"We'll both have a coffee and one of those little apple pie things," Bernie said.

"The mini *tarte tatins* do look delicious," Angie added.

"I'll just have a coffee," Henry said.

"Me, too," Randy said and stood up. He whispered in Lana's ear, "I'm just going to the men's room. Unless you need some help?"

"Nope, I've got this," she said with a smile, hoping he wouldn't take long. Her mind was spinning through all of the facts she had learned about Chad, Bernie, Sabine, and Miranda, making it difficult to concentrate on her guests' needs. There was something she was forgetting, something important, but she couldn't for the life of her remember what it was.

When she placed their order, the server grabbed a coffee cup and said, "I can make your drinks now. But the dessert plates are in the dishwasher. It will be a few minutes before we can serve the cake," the woman apologized.

"Oh, that's okay. Just wave when they're ready and I'll come over and get them."

When the server had filled the tray with the four coffees, Lana picked it up. "Let me take these over and come back for the rest. I don't want to spill them all."

Lana balanced the tray and slowly turned around, almost bumping into Miranda.

"Need some help?" her guest asked.

Lana had to force herself not to act differently, for fear of tipping her hand. The more she thought about Chad and his future plans, the more she suspected that Miranda had something to do with his demise. But until she knew for certain whether Miranda had known about his move to New York and until she figured out how she could have poisoned him, it was all conjecture. Until then, she had to pretend as if nothing had changed.

"That would be wonderful, thank you," Lana said, as brightly as she could.

"I'll take these coffees over, if you don't mind waiting on the teas?"

"Sure thing," Miranda said.

Lana served the coffees to her guests, then walked back towards the counter to return the tray. The server was returning from the hot water boiler with the last cup of tea in her hand. As soon as she placed it onto the tray, Miranda walked back to their table, smiling at Lana as she went.

When Lana returned, Randy was crossing back to their group, as well. Her tea was already on the table. The heat rising from the cup swirled in the cool air. She took a tentative sip. It was a touch sour, but didn't have a strong taste otherwise.

"Chad didn't like to drink it with anything added, but I do really think it is much nicer with honey." Miranda handed her a pot of honey, already on the table. "You really should try it."

Lana added a heavy spoonful, then sipped her hot drink. It was quite delicious. She blew on the surface in order to cool it, eager to drink more.

Randy picked up his cup and raised it in the air. "To our wonderful group and this glorious day," he said.

"I'll drink to that," Henry said, holding his wife close. For the first time since this tour began, the couple had spent the entire day together, and both seemed happier for it. Maybe Randy was right; they did need more Miranda-free days in their lives.

Wondering where the cake was, Lana went over to ask the server, who explained that they didn't have enough chocolate torte left and one of her colleagues had gone to get more. Luckily this café had three locations spread throughout the gardens, meaning it wouldn't take but a few minutes. Lana looked to her watch; they had been here for fifteen minutes already, half of their break. Lana hoped their local guide wasn't in a hurry. The server must have noticed, because she offered her excuses and made another round of drinks, to make up for the delay.

Her guests didn't seem to mind. Lana finished her first cup of tea in one swig, then poured honey into the second one. She would have to make hibiscus tea more often; it was quite refreshing.

As they waited for their cake to be dished up, her guests chatted about their favorite rooms in the main palace and the over-the-top decorations and furnishings. Lana still couldn't believe how big it was. *How many servants did it take to keep the place clean?* she mused.

"I can't wait to see Marie Antoinette's private residence. That Queen's Hamlet looks like something out of an English fairy tale," Miranda said.

"Our guide did say that both she and her husband were completely cut off from the harsh realities of daily life in their time. She built her hamlet as a place to escape into her own little fantasy world," Angie added.

"As if shutting herself off from the world solved her problems," Miranda muttered, her tone oddly bitter.

"I wouldn't call anything about this place little," Henry exclaimed, getting a chuckle out of the group. "And they didn't have social media or twenty-four-hour news channels like they do now. The king and queen would have been dependent on their advisors to keep them up to date."

"That's a good point, Henry," his wife said. "I find it so hard to believe that cellphones and the internet didn't exist when we were born. I can't even remember what it was like not to be connected all the time. I wouldn't survive the day without my phone."

If Miranda did poison Chad, how did she do it? And when? Lana half-listened to her group, while her mind chewed through the possibilities. She sipped her second cup of tea as she looked out at the gardens, letting her eyes get lost in the symmetry of the plantings and severity of the manicuring. Sunlight broke through the clouds, reflecting off a small pond, in the middle of which stood the Temple of Love. A group of tourists stopped close to the circular, neoclassical structure and sat down on the grass, turning their faces to the sun. Lana wondered whether the fish enjoyed sunbathing, too.

Randy's voice broke through her thoughts. "Hey Lana, I see our cake is ready. Shall I go get it?"

Lana looked over at her fellow guide. "Sure, buddy, that would be great." When Randy started to rise, Lana touched his arm. "What do you think, Randy? Can fish get sunburned?"

He looked at her quizzically, then laughed. "That's a great question. I never stopped to consider it before. Let me think about it while I get the cake."

"Roger and out."

"Are you feeling okay, Lana?" Randy put a hand on her shoulder, concern in his voice.

"Sure, never better," she responded with a smile, sipping her tea as she gazed at the pond.

The porcelain plate clinking against the table drew Lana's attention back to her group. She stared into her torte, a French specialty, her eyes getting lost in the darkness of the chocolate.

"Let them eat cake," she muttered, recalling Marie Antoinette's line and Miranda laughing about it. Lana went white as she stared at the cake before her. Ever since Chad's death, she had been so focused on the baguettes, dips, and tea that she had forgotten about the cheesecake Sabine brought along and the extra berries Miranda added to Chad's slice. The belladonna berries were the same size as blueberries, and their darker color would have been disguised by the chocolate sauce Sabine poured over their desserts.

Lana's eyes widened to saucers. Miranda had the motive and opportunity. She could have easily added poisonous berries to his cheesecake at the picnic, right in front of everyone. And none of them were the wiser. "Oh no," Lana moaned.

"Lana, are you okay?" Randy asked. "Your eyes look funny."

"I feel nauseated. All this walking and we have barely eaten; I think my blood sugar level is dropping. Do you mind watching the group? I better go to the bathroom," she said, rising from her chair. Randy caught it as it started to tip over.

"We'll wait for you here," he said.

"Great," Lana responded, already weaving her way off of the terrace and towards the toilet. She had to call the inspector and tell him about Miranda, Chad, and the berries. Once she rounded the corner of the café and was out of her group's sightline, Lana pulled out her telephone. She tried to unlock the screen, but her eyes wouldn't focus. She leaned against the wall and felt her forehead. It was covered in sweat. *It must be the shock of discovering one of my clients is a killer*, Lana thought. Before she could try to dial the police investigator's number, she felt a hand on her elbow.

169

"Oh, you poor thing. Shall I help you?" Miranda asked, concern in her voice as she took Lana's phone out of her hand. "A walk will do you good." Miranda grabbed her arm and propelled her onto the closest garden path, walking away from the terrace.

Lana tried to reach for her phone, but her arm wasn't cooperating.

"What's wrong? Aren't you feeling well?" Miranda smiled as she led them farther away from the café.

With each step, Lana's dizziness worsened. Soon she was seeing double. "I'm going to throw up," Lana choked.

"You don't want to ruin these incredible gardens, do you?" Miranda pulled her roughly along the path, keeping her away from the other tourists milling about.

"Did you put something in my tea?"

"The same Gelsemium I put in Chad's hibiscus tea. Though this time I didn't make the mistake of being too stingy. The belladonna berries were supposed to be the backup. Their sourness suited him better, anyway," Miranda said, her tone bright. When they reached a bench far from the café, Miranda patted her arm and smiled at a passerby. "Shall we sit?"

Lana's body dropped onto the cold stone bench as Miranda jerked her down.

"Why did Chad have to die?" she asked, her speech slurred.

"I think you know that," Miranda said. "His deal with *The New Yorker* went through. He lied and told me it had fallen apart. If I hadn't found his change-of-address forms, filled in with his new apartment's address, I wouldn't have known what he was planning."

"But you didn't have to divorce..." Lana said, her sentence trailing off.

"Chad refused to agree to a separation and demanded a divorce so that he could start afresh. He said he would go to the church and ask for an annulment if I didn't agree. Can you believe the nerve? But you know what stings most? When I wanted to attend Juilliard, he refused to move to New York. I gave up my chance at acting school and to have children, only to appease him, and now he needs space to follow his dreams? All I wanted was his love and respect. But he was going to sneak away without even telling me. That spineless weasel had no right to treat me so badly." Miranda kept a smile on her face and her voice cheery.

"You know what really got me? Chad didn't want to spoil our trip by telling me he was moving to New York next week. He was going to tell me after we flew home." A tear rolled down her cheek, possibly the first real sign of emotion she had shown this entire trip.

She pointed to a statue when a couple strolled by, continuing to speak only when they were out of view. "It was easy enough to add the belladonna berries to his cake. Some food critic; he didn't even notice them. It's too bad you found out about his new column. You only had to stay out of my business for two more days, and you would have survived."

Lana fell forward, unable to keep her body upright. Miranda pulled her back up and leaned her into the corner of the bench, then took sunglasses out of her bag and put them on Lana. She bent down and whispered, "I am going to leave you now. Sorry about this. I hope it's painless."

Miranda stood up as Randy jogged up the path. "Lana? Are you out here?" Unfortunately, he didn't see them among all of the tourists milling about. "Lana Hansen of Wanderlust Tours, are you here?" he called out again, his voice fading as he moved farther away.

Miranda ran in the opposite direction of Randy's voice. Lana tried to raise her arm, but only her shoulder seemed to respond. A tear trickled down her face as she gurgled Randy's name. There was no way he could hear her. She was going to die in Versailles. The thought drove a soft scream out of her lungs, loud enough to attract a group of nearby tourists' attention, just before she fell face-first onto the gravel-strewn path.

"Call an ambulance! This woman is having seizures!" one of them screamed.

Several people raced over to her, Randy included. "Where's Miranda?"

Lana tried to respond but couldn't speak. Her brain was spinning. She tried to sit up, but she couldn't control her muscles. Tremors took hold of her as Randy yelled again for help. Every part of her body burned and ached. Lana let her eyelids droop shut, willing death to take her quickly, as Randy's face hovered above hers. Her fellow guide slapped her cheek and screamed her name. The last thing Lana remembered was him shoving his fingers down her throat, then only darkness.

32

Perfect Day for a Picnic

February 28—Seattle, Washington

Lana raised a cup of tea to her lips, savoring the smells and flavors of the earthy mint. The sun was shining, there was only a slight breeze, and it was a balmy sixty-five degrees. It was a perfect day for a picnic.

Lana looked across the blanket at Jane, mixing together a bean dish while Willow poured Randy tea. Lana was so glad to be alive and well enough to enjoy this glorious day with her friends at Gas Works Park. It was her first outing since being released from a Parisian hospital six days earlier, and it felt as if Seattle wanted to welcome her back.

Thanks to Randy's quick thinking, Lana had survived her brush with death. By forcing her to throw up, he was able to get most of the Gelsemium out of her system, and the paramedics pumped out the rest. Otherwise, she would have been a goner.

Luckily, service was quite slow at the café in Versailles, meaning the police found Lana's empty cup with the Gelsemium still in it, before the waitstaff had cleared their table. It turned out that Miranda had spent enough time alone at the counter, while the server poured teas, to add Gelsemium to Lana's cup. She had been carrying around a ziplock bag full of the deadly leaves and berries since their trip to the Jardin des Plantes.

This time, though, Miranda couldn't frame Pierre le Monde or her friend

Sabine. Miranda was quite the actress, but Lana's poisoned cup was the smoking gun that broke through her lies.

After being confronted with all of the evidence, Miranda finally admitted to poisoning both Lana's tea with Gelsemium and her husband's cheesecake with belladonna berries during the picnic. In the confusion that ensued once Chad began convulsing at the picnic, she had managed to add a few to Jane's berry-yogurt dip, as well. It was one of the many red herrings Miranda had thrown into the mix during their week in Paris.

Apparently she had been planning Chad's murder since finding change-of-address forms in his desk drawer, weeks before their departure for Paris. Her acting abilities were put to good use during the market tour and picnic. Randy's quick thinking not only saved Lana's life, but also ensured Miranda would pay for her crimes.

"Say, Lana and Randy, did either one of you get your invitation from Sabine yet?" Willow asked.

"Not that I'm aware of. But I did forget to check my mailbox this morning. An invitation to what?" Lana asked.

"She sent an email to my yoga studio, asking for our addresses. She and Henry are renewing their vows, and we are all invited."

Lana couldn't believe her ears. "Are you kidding me? After how badly the week went in Paris, I figured our guests would never want to see me, or each other, again."

"*Au contraire.* It's because of Paris that they decided to do this. Sabine wasn't even aware that she was abandoning Henry to help Miranda. Henry said that shortly after they married, Miranda and Chad began having problems and Miranda started showing up at their house at all hours. Sabine was so used to putting Miranda first, she didn't consider that Henry might be resentful of all the attention she was giving to her friend. It opened her eyes, in more ways than one, I imagine," Jane answered.

"Sabine thought she was being a good friend to Miranda by helping her arrange the plants tour and baking workshop. They'd relied on each other for so long. Miranda took advantage of their friendship, once she knew Chad was leaving her," Randy added. He had been right all along; Miranda was a manipulator and Sabine her favorite target. It was only too bad that Chad had to die and Miranda be arrested before their unhealthy pattern could be broken.

"I wonder if Bernie and Angie are invited," Lana said.

"Yep. Bernie stopped by yesterday to let me know they'd gotten theirs already. His new conveyor belt restaurant is opening about a block away from my studio, can you believe it! Seattle is so small," Willow laughed. "And Angie signed up for one of my afternoon classes. I'm so glad; I really like her."

"I do, too," Jane replied, to Lana's surprise. They may not have gotten off on the right foot, but both couples did seem to be becoming friends by the end of the trip.

Lana shook her head, thinking about how things had ended up all right, despite all of the chaos and hardship during the tour.

She held up her cup. "This glorious day deserves a toast. To Paris," she said with a grin as the others groaned.

"How about to good friends?" Randy suggested.

"I'll toast to that," Lana said, clinking her glass against his. Randy had proved to be a great friend. After leading their group through their last day and to the airport, he'd stayed on in Paris, chit-chatting with Lana to keep the boredom at bay.

It had taken her three days to recover enough to be allowed to fly back. Lana had gladly conversed with him the entire flight home, grateful he had put his life on hold to help her out. She was also glad his girlfriend was so understanding.

Her next scheduled tour didn't leave for a week. At Dotty's insistence, she'd had a checkup with her local doctor as soon as she returned, who gave Lana her blessing to go back to work, providing she took it easy until departure time. Lana was happy to oblige. *Life rushes by fast enough*, she thought, *it's good to just enjoy the moment.*

"I propose a toast to Rose," Willow said, a grin splitting her face.

"Or Johnathan," Jane added, meeting Willow's glass in the air.

Lana looked at her friends, puzzled. "Who are they?"

175

"Our top baby names. Our first IVF appointment is next week," Willow said.

Lana squealed and hugged her friends tight. "You two are going to make great parents! I hope it all works out. So what change made this happen?"

"I took on a partner," Jane said, "We went to medical school together. She's an incredible doctor, and I'm lucky she wants to join my practice. She'll be working three days a week, starting next month. Meaning I'll be working four days a week instead of seven."

Lana's jaw dropped in shock. "Are you serious? That is wonderful news!"

"And I'm hiring more instructors and canceling those early morning classes," Willow added. "They are always the hardest to fill, anyway."

"Congratulations, both of you. Whatever happens with the IVF, it's good you are making each other a priority," Lana said, then added, with a mischievous smile, "You know you have a built-in grandma. Dotty is going to freak out."

"And an Auntie Lana, we hope," Willow said. "If it all works out. We're going to assume the worst until I actually get pregnant."

Lana looked at her friends, smiling at each other. They were so happy they were glowing. Someday she would find someone who would make her feel the same way. Until she did, Lana felt incredibly grateful to have good friends to share her life with.

THE END

Thank you for reading my novel!
Reviews really do help readers decide whether they want to take a chance on a new author. If you enjoyed this story, please consider posting a review on BookBub, Goodreads, or with your favorite retailer.
I appreciate it! Jennifer S. Alderson

Follow the further adventures of Lana Hansen in *Death by Windmill: A Mother's Day Murder in Amsterdam*—Book Three of the Travel Can Be Murder Mystery Series!

A Mother's Day trip to the Netherlands turns deadly when a guest plummets from a windmill. Was it an accident or a murder? For Lana Hansen, the answer will mean freedom or imprisonment for someone close to her...

Wanderlust Tours guide Lana Hansen and her mother, Gillian, haven't seen eye to eye in over a decade, ever since Lana was wrongly fired from her job as an investigative reporter. So when Lana's boss invites Gillian to join her upcoming Mother's Day tour to the Netherlands, Lana is less than pleased.

What could be worse than spending ten days with her estranged mother? Lana is about to find out...

The tour begins on a high note when the majority of guests bond during their visit to the Keukenhof flower gardens and a cruise around the picturesque canals of Amsterdam.

Despite her initial reservations, Lana thinks this might be the best group she had ever led. Until she discovers one of her guests—a recent retiree named Priscilla—is the person who destroyed her career in journalism.

All Lana can see is red. But circumstances dictate that she figure out a way to lead the tour, make peace with her mother, and not murder her guest. She doesn't know whether she can handle the pressure.

Lana needn't worry. Shortly after their fight, Priscilla falls off the balcony of a historic windmill at Zaanse Schans. Was she pushed or simply careless? The investigating officers suspect murder—and topping their suspect list is Lana's mom!

Can Lana save Gillian? Or will her mother end up spending the rest of her days in a Dutch prison?

You can buy the eBook or paperback version of *Death by Windmill* at your favorite retailer.

Or flip to the end of this book to read Chapter One of *Death by Windmill* now!

Acknowledgments

I am deeply indebted to my husband and son for their support and encouragement while I wrote, researched, and edited *Death by Baguette*.

Many thanks to editor Sadye Scott-Hainchek for making this novel shine.

Paris is a favorite city of mine, and I have visited it several times over the span of sixteen years. It's a city that is static, yet constantly evolving, and every trip brings a new, splendid experience.

All of the locations referred to in this novel are real, and I have done my best to describe them accurately. The only intentional exception is the greenhouse Lana's group visits at the Jardin des Plantes. The real Garden of Resource Plants (or Garden of Useful Plants, depending on which sources you check) is planted in the outdoor beds, yet my group visits in the winter, so I moved it into one of the existing greenhouses. I also took liberties with my descriptions of this garden, making it more deadly than the real one.

Bon voyage!

About the Author

Jennifer S. Alderson was born in San Francisco, grew up in Seattle, and currently lives in Amsterdam. After traveling extensively around Asia, Oceania, and Central America, she lived in Darwin, Australia, before settling in the Netherlands.

Jennifer's love of travel, art, and culture inspires her award-winning Zelda Richardson Mystery series, her Travel Can Be Murder Cozy Mysteries, and her Carmen De Luca Art Sleuth Mysteries. Her background in art history, journalism, and multimedia development enriches her novels.

When not writing, she can be found perusing a museum, biking around Amsterdam, or enjoying a coffee along the canal while planning her next research trip.

For more information about the author and her upcoming novels, please visit Jennifer's website [http://jennifersalderson.com].

Books by Jennifer S. Alderson:

Carmen De Luca Art Mysteries
Collecting Can Be Murder
A Statue To Die For
Forgeries and Fatalities
A Killer Inheritance

Travel Can Be Murder Cozy Mysteries
Death on the Danube: A New Year's Murder in Budapest
Death by Baguette: A Valentine's Day Murder in Paris

Death by Windmill: A Mother's Day Murder in Amsterdam
Death by Bagpipes: A Summer Murder in Edinburgh
Death by Fountain: A Christmas Murder in Rome
Death by Leprechaun: A Saint Patrick's Day Murder in Dublin
Death by Flamenco: An Easter Murder in Seville
Death by Gondola: A Springtime Murder in Venice
Death by Puffin: A Bachelorette Party Murder in Reykjavik

Zelda Richardson Art Mysteries
The Lover's Portrait: An Art Mystery
Rituals of the Dead: An Artifact Mystery
Marked for Revenge: An Art Heist Thriller
The Vermeer Deception: An Art Mystery

Standalone Travel Thriller
Down and Out in Kathmandu: A Backpacker Mystery

Death by Windmill: A Mother's Day Murder in Amsterdam

Chapter One: Mothers and Daughters

March 20—Seattle, Washington

"Are you one hundred percent positive that Gillian won't mind you working on Mother's Day?" Dotty Thompson asked. From her tone, it was evident that she did not believe a word Lana Hansen was saying.

Dotty was finalizing her roster of guides for several upcoming tours and was now wishy-washy about allowing Lana to lead the Mother's Day tour of the Netherlands. Since recently discovering that Lana and her mother were estranged, Dotty had made it her mission to bring them back together and seemed to think the upcoming holiday was the perfect time to do so. As much as Lana loved Dotty, she was having a tough time figuring out how to tell the older lady to butt out.

"I am quite certain. We haven't celebrated the day together in several years. Ten, to be exact," Lana replied. Even though they lived only a few miles apart, her mother could have lived in Alaska for all it mattered. They never made time for each other, and Lana was the first to admit that both were to blame.

Dotty leaned against her apple tree, recovering from the shock. Dotty's pug and Jack Russell terrier chose that moment to play tug-of-war with one of the colorful paper streamers strewn across the lawn. As they growled and shook their jaws, bits of the decorations flew off, sending a shower of rainbow-colored confetti across the lawn.

Lana groaned in irritation. Their playfulness was only making it more

182

difficult to clean up after last night's spring equinox party. Dotty's backyard had been filled with neighbors happy to ring in the return of spring with a glass of bubbly and finger foods, while their children ran and played among Dotty's fruit trees.

"Okay, boys, that's enough." Lana tried to wrestle the colorful streamer out of the dogs' mouths, but they misinterpreted her attempt to clean up as playtime. They growled and yelped as she slowly loosened the decorations from their muzzles. After Lana had taken away their toy, the two dogs moved on to tag, yapping in delight as they chased each other around the yard.

Lana's cat, Seymour, rubbed against her leg, purring as he watched the dogs play. When Seymour sniffed a tiny scrap of paper and tentatively tasted it, Lana shooed him away and redoubled her cleaning efforts.

"Besides, I have always wanted to visit the Netherlands, and you already have me scheduled to lead it. Please don't ground me. It won't force me to look Gillian up. We haven't spoken in so long, she wouldn't be expecting me to get in touch, even on Mother's Day," Lana pleaded.

"I cannot believe you haven't celebrated Mother's Day with Gillian in over a decade." Dotty shook her head slowly, seemingly stuck on Lana's initial answer. "She is your *mother*, after all. And you both live in Seattle, for goodness' sake."

Lana shrugged. "We were never close. After I got fired from the newspaper, our contact dissipated pretty quickly. I think she is ashamed to admit that I am her daughter." One look at Dotty's distraught expression made her add, "I can't blame her; Gillian's world is advertising and perception. After the *Seattle Chronicle* lost the libel suit and fired me, I was in the news a lot, but never in a positive light."

Lana closed her eyes, recalling those dark days. Soon after she had been sacked, her mother had stopped taking Lana's calls. Gillian was her only relative on the West Coast, which made her rejection even more painful. Her father's family was spread across the East Coast and she had lost touch with most of them since her dad's death twenty years ago.

Dotty pulled Lana in for a hug. "Her job doesn't give her an excuse to leave you high and dry. How could she not love you? You are so smart, creative, and rational. If you were my flesh and blood, I would tell everyone I met how wonderful you are."

"Sometimes I wish you were my biological mother, Dotty," Lana confessed, relaxing into the older lady's embrace. They had only lived under the same roof for a year, but most days, Dotty felt more like her mother than Gillian ever had.

"It's just not right." Dotty shook her head sadly.

"Giving birth to a child is not a guarantee that you will become best friends, Dotty," Lana gently reminded her.

Lana knew not being able to have children was a cross Dotty bore. She was a wonderful stepmother to six grown sons, but on Mother's Day, the kids always treated their biological mothers to breakfast, not Dotty. For Dotty, it was one of the most painful days of the year. Lana's only regret in leading this tour was that she wouldn't be in Seattle on Mother's Day to help brighten up her friend's day.

"If you are sure Gillian won't mind, then you are welcome to be the lead guide on the Holland tour. Since only women have booked spaces, I did ask Randy to be the second guide. I figure you could use a little testosterone on the trip," Dotty cackled.

Lana sighed in relief. "Thanks, Dotty."

She was really looking forward to seeing the Netherlands and, in particular, Amsterdam. The historic windmills, many canals, grand homes, and plethora of bicycles seemed so romantic and charming. It would also be fun to work with Randy again. He was one of the most laid-back guides employed by Wanderlust Tours at the moment. After bonding during a tour in France, they had gotten together regularly when both were back in Seattle. Lana also got along well with his girlfriend, Gloria, a spunky Italian beauty who was a beehive of activity and positivity that was perfect for him. Lana wouldn't be surprised if they tied the knot later this year.

Most of all, Lana was glad this trip gave her a good excuse not to get together with Gillian. After not speaking for almost two years, her mother had recently begun following Lana's social media accounts. In Gillian's world, this was a way of saying hello. So far, Lana had ignored her and not followed her back or acknowledged her likes. Lana hadn't told Dotty about this recent surge of activity for fear that she would ground her until she and Gillian met face to face. *If Gillian really wanted to talk to me, she could pick up the phone,* Lana thought, as she tied off one garbage bag and grabbed another.

* * *

Are you enjoying the book so far? Why not buy *Death by Windmill* now at your favorite retailer and keep reading! Available as paperback, eBook, and in Kindle Unlimited.